NEW WRITINGS IN SF 28

is now one of the most well-established and respected series in the science fiction world. Created in 1964 by John Carnell, in collaboration with Corgi Books, NEW WRITINGS rapidly gained a reputation as a showcase for the most talented writers in the field; and when John Carnell died in 1972 the series was taken over by Kenneth Bulmer whose wide-ranging knowledge of, and enthusiasm for SF has continued to make NEW WRITINGS the place to find stories of a speculative, forward-looking, and mind-provoking nature, highlighting and illustrating the dilemmas of today – and tomorrow.

In the same series edited by JOHN CARNELL

NEW WRITINGS IN SF 1–21

and edited by KENNETH BULMER

NEW WRITINGS IN SF 22–27

and published by Corgi Books

New Writings in SF 28

Edited by Kenneth Bulmer

CORGI BOOKS
A DIVISION OF TRANSWORLD PUBLISHERS LTD

NEW WRITINGS IN SF 28

A CORGI BOOK 0 552 10527 9

Originally published in Great Britain by
Sidgwick and Jackson Limited.

PRINTING HISTORY
Sidgwick and Jackson edition published 1976
Corgi edition published 1977

This book is set in Linotype Pilgrim

Corgi Books are published by
Transworld Publishers Ltd,
Century House, 61–63 Uxbridge Road,
Ealing, London W5 5SA
Made and printed in Great Britain by
Cox & Wyman Ltd., London, Reading and Fakenham

CONTENTS

FOREWORD

by

KENNETH BULMER

ONE of the delights of editing a collection of short stories is the discovery of a superb story just at the moment when the editor is convinced that there is no one left in the whole wide world who can write apart from those respected and reliable authors whose names have graced past volumes.

Since the inception of New Writings in SF, more than ten years ago, as a showcase for new and original work in the sf field that would appeal to a wider audience, many new writers have made their mark in its pages. Just how many new readers have come to a refreshing discovery and appreciation of sf in that time it would be difficult to say. Exactly how many of them have gone on to become writers is even more complicated to judge, for so many components go to the makeup of a working writer that to trace individual sources of motivation and inspiration demands lengthy scholarship so far not undertaken.

But the delight in reading a first-class story by an 'unknown' name is always immense. Very often the writer turns out to be a polished practitioner in other, non sf, fields; the 'unknown' is unknown only to sf. To take the interesting case of lady writers in New Writings – I doubt they'd thank me for calling them authoresses – Volume 24 saw Cherry Wilder's widely acclaimed THE ARK OF JAMES CARLYLE. I am happy to report that this story saw republication in Australia's very first sf short story anthology, 'Beyond Tomorrow', edited by Lee Harding. The book was published to coincide with Australia's first World Science Fiction Convention, and the hope is that it will be the beginning of an indigenous series to the benefit of Ozwriters. Vera Johnson, whose barbed and thought-provoking THE DAY THEY CUT OFF THE POWER appeared in New Writings 27, has been singing and strumming from success to success, and I would draw your attention to her L.P. 'Bald Eagle', recorded live at the Black Horse Folk Club, from Sweet Folk All Recordings Ltd.

It has been suggested that one of the differences between pre-nineteenth century literature and that which follows is that the former had to look for change in a spatial direction, whilst the latter could find it in a temporal. If this is true of mundane literature it is particularly true of one kind of sf and the literature of the imagination. In the old days change was so slow that to perceive it for the purposes of fiction with any kind of relevant immediacy one had to travel to another country or a fantasy world behind the moon. With sociological and scientific change increasing visibly in tempo, one has only to wait to perceive changes whirling along in the debris of time.

So the story-submissions that come across my desk and the time-travelling editor at last reach a nodal point. One's faith in the continuing good health of writing is re-established.

The first story in this volume is by the third lady writer to grace the pages of New Writings in SF. WHAT HAPPENED TO WILLIAM COOMBES is written with great style and distinction and captures a very great deal of the underlying unease of our culture, inter alia. This is one to treasure. As for Mr. Coombes himself, a most realistically-conceived old gentleman, it occurs to me that the readership may consider Angela Rogers to have been too hard on the old fellow, or too disbelieving of her own powers, about his final happening.

Graham Leman's story may strike a few chords out of its time-span; but once again sf is shown to be a master-medium in which humour can be employed in dealing with a sobering malaise of modern life. Brian Aldiss is a writer who likes to go out and cut down the tall grass. And if he can lay his hands on a good scythe he will use that in preference to a little half-moon sickle. The name Aldiss appears on very many of the books generally considered by sf people to be in the very top class, those they would choose to be space-wrecked with. There is a good chance that THE BONES OF BERTRAND RUSSELL may receive its premier at some upcoming world convention, and no prizes are offered for cast lists made up from your pet loves or aversions in the sf world.

Robert Holdstock presents us with a story that appears to be one thing whilst actually being something entirely different. The single item that may bother most people about Mr. Holdstock will, inevitably, be – does Mr. Holdstock keep Mrs. Holdstock in the closet? Like Robert Holdstock, Leroy Kettle has recently gone free-lancing, and his THE GREAT PLAN, a provocative story in which the writer's well-known aversion to work is given a solid substratum of speculation, augurs well for his success in his chosen profession, and one looks forward to examples of Leroy Kettle's handling of humour in the sf context. Bryn Fortey deals much more directly with the writer's problems, and, incidentally, comes up with a beautiful notion in Black Art. May I add, on a personal note, that almost all Bryn Fortey has to say about editors is just about ninety nine percent accurate – if not in this world then in the one he posits here.

With THE SEAFARER in New Writings 26, Ritchie Smith and Thomas Penman made their debut as professional science fiction writers. Now they present BY THE BANKS OF THE NILE which is just as rich and exotic, filled with the iron clangour and decadent luxury of a future age consciously drawing upon the past and bending it to the unyielding demands of that future. This story marks a positive step forward, as was suggested in their own words quoted in the foreword to volume 26.

Manuel van Loggem is a distinguished novelist of his native country, the Netherlands, and we are privileged to see his work here. This arose as a result of our meeting in Gent, and he has since visited sf gatherings in this country where his urbane appearance gave no inkling of the trenchancy of his conversation. The two aspects mingle most happily in the bite of THE CALL OF THE WILD. E. C. Tubb's story can be seen as companion piece to his EVANE in New Writings 22, which was selected for the ANNUAL WORLD'S BEST SF anthology published by DAWBooks of New York.

Michael Stall is extending his mastery of different areas of the sf field, for THE FIVE DOORS, RICE BRANDY and his present work herein presented, MANGANON, are all very different in tone and colour and in their emphases. With MANGANON Michael Stall transports us to a macabre world that is the subject of high-level thinking presented in an academically scientific fashion, quite different – as Michael Stall points out – from the actuality, where passion and blood must appear in close-up to participants for whom the author arouses like feelings.

These ten stories, all new, three by writers new to New Writings in SF, continue the idea of the series, that of presenting a variety of sf themes to a wide audience as well as to lovers of sf of many years' standing.

Kenneth Bulmer.

WHAT HAPPENED TO WILLIAM COOMBES

by

ANGELA ROGERS

*The pattern existed, it was there, waiting to be deciphered;
but what happened to Mr. Coombes demanded belief beyond
mere credulity. After all, cats do survive, they prowl down
plastic corridors as if they were in living jungle. They might
touch the dust of Mars, really touch it, that is, and not just
sense the feeling of it through plastic space-suit gloves. What
Angela Rogers has to say in this articulate and intensively
evocative and sensitive story is probably not best summed
up in her last line; but, then again, perhaps that is really
what happened to William Coombes. I do not think so myself, and I fancy neither will you, at the end . . .*

WHAT HAPPENED TO WILLIAM COOMBES

WHEN William Coombes was a boy he thought that he could escape from enclosure into space. He ate his good food in the meal hall with his back pressed against another back and other arms brushing his, and watched soup run down the chin of the girl he faced. Or he lay awake next to his sleeping brother and heard each slight breath against the murmur of his parents' voices and the continual soft sounds of people: walking past in the corridors, or turning on taps, or suddenly laughing behind their own unnoticed walls. He endured it easily because he knew he would stand alone on Mars and look across empty land to the horizon, or kneel and put his hand on the ground itself and dig his fingers into the sand.

On his fifteenth birthday he enlisted and within six years he did stand alone on Mars and look at space through a faceplate. And he knelt quite easily in his flexible suiting and let handfuls of sand run through his fingers. What he touched was not sand but his protecting gloves.

He learned that man is an animal adapted to live on Earth, and that when he pretends to leave it he must carry Earth with him in small, economical packets. He found that Earth on Mars was a cluster of pressure domes as clean and crowded as a Woburn community block, with the immigration programme always one step ahead of the expansion schedule. When he tried to walk away from Earth into Mars he could not. He was an alien in a space suit, still carrying his skin of Earth in a little envelope; not so economical as a dome but smaller, very small.

He came to think of himself as physically tied to Earth, but by a running noose. He had stood on roofs in Woburn and felt himself lost in the distances of the universe; but soaring between planes he was only aware of bulkheads and pressure margins and cubic centimetres of occupied space. And it took months from his life to move from one inner planet to another; years to visit Neptune; a lifetime probably to pass the bounds of the Solar system. Since he was trapped, it came to seem perverse to let himself live and die in small traps within a trap, and Earth itself grew in his mind.

He stayed with SPEC for thirty years. He was based with Supply, and spent most of the years doing social maths in small rooms. He was at Archangel for twelve years, Oban for three, Mauiai for six. He saw a lot of the world on short postings, but altogether he spent less than six years off-Earth: usually doing the same work in similar rooms. He had an unusual knack for logistics and moved up through the groups at great speed. That surprised me when he first mentioned it; but after seventeen years of Mr. Coombes' reminiscences I know that Space Administration is mostly logistics and the supply of tranquilizers.

Yet he did extraordinary things. He helped to build the *Alpha Centauri*; stacked the colonists, and saw it drift away from the Sun towards the dark. He was nearly assassinated on Mercury during the riots, or thought it wise to say so. He trained before the Eight Hour War of course, when things were opulent, and during one month he was taken again and again in a small winged transport high above the buildings, miles, he said, and told to jump into the air. Time after time he stepped out of the transport into the wind and swam above the earth, in a sense falling and yet afloat. At a certain height above the roofs he had to pull a cord and a parachute would snap him back to safety. That was before he got to Mars and he pulled the cord always without question, even with relief.

Over the years he told me a lot about his life in SPEC, but for him the life was mainly logistics. He only mentioned what I would call adventures in passing, although he did talk of the training falls many times, and he returned obsessively to the experiments in Parker, and what happened to Rachel Kwe.

Venus is so inimical we don't even mine there now; but in Mr. Coombes' time they still hoped to colonize. It took three tries to establish Parker, and when they did get it up they were held behind its walls. They shipped in autoprobes and began to survey, but the write-off rate was too high and there was strong pressure to try one or other of the human adaption techniques which various groups were working on.

Mr. Coombes told me that they should have tried clones; but all work on clones had been banned after the Darkside riots. None of the alternatives was really viable, but they gave the contract to Unichem for a scheme which was no better conceived than the others, but was rather less ambitious. Probably someone said 'Conservative', and someone else 'Ah! Safe'. So Unichem set up a unit at Parker and advertised for subjects.

William Coombes should have known better, but he imagined himself wading away from the squat domes of Parker into an unspoiled world, and he would have volunteered. He only had two years left to serve, but by that time he was a Marshall, and acting as Supply Co-ordinator to the settlements, so he couldn't get a clearance. He worked out his time, but he was obsessed with the experiments on Venus. He transferred his own control unit to Parker, which was substandard and so plagued by contamination alerts that they slept in their suits, and he waited on the project.

Unichem hoped to replace their subjects' skin tissues with flexibly segmented carapaces similar to some successfully grown on Barbary apes. The Barbary tissue seemed to be completely impervious to the corrosive Venusian atmosphere, and impressively resistant to termites. It seemed at least possible that it would withstand High Zone pressures, and a most ingenious sub-cutaneous cooling process was also being discussed. There were problems. For a start men are not clinically interchangeable with Barbary apes. Then the impermeable carapace could not perform the normal functions of the skin, which had in some way to be continued artificially. Again, it was considered necessary to seal off all orifices except the nose and mouth. This required the replacement of the digestive and the destruction of the reproductive systems.

The end in view was a man who could travel with only an air pack and a cooling unit. He would be fed intravenously at base, and his blood would be washed clean as he slept. There would have been little purpose to it if they had succeeded.

Although the experiments were irresponsible, they were carried out with great care, so that when the first subject died only six had been processed at all, and the last one of those escaped relatively undamaged. The woman named Rachel Kwe was also still alive when Mr. Coombes left, but they had gone too far with her to be able to do more than keep her alive.

Rachel Kwe lived at that time in a plexiglass tank which was filled with a clear glutinous liquid in which she could move freely if slowly. Her head was encased in a bubble helmet from which a welter of pipes and cables ran up out of the liquid to a life support system above the tank. They had not attempted to grow the new tissue on her because they knew that it would kill her, but they had already spoiled her for the air of Earth, so she was trapped there.

He saw her once. She was drifting loosely upright in the middle of the tank; her body wasted, silvery and hairless; her face in its smaller case brown and impassive; her eyes closed. He had been told that she would ignore him; but when he had watched her for a long time her eyes opened and she looked at him and knew him. She drifted to the glass and her lips moved and the little speaker set in the tank said 'Marshall', and she put out her shadow hand and placed it on the glass as if to touch him. The glass was warm.

His face could only have shown despair. They looked at each other through the glass until the little speaker said 'It would have been worse anyway', while her lips moved and her eyes closed, and he turned away.

That was more than twenty years ago. Mr. Coombes was discharged and came home to Woburn. Rachel Kwe died no doubt. Mr. Coombes was made Supply Officer then Manager at the Hockliff Plant, which like most plants at that time was damaged, obsolescent, and overburdened. It still is in fact, if you substitute the damage from twenty years' wear for the damage from war, but we haven't starved since he took over. We lived for four months on a kind of raw green gulp during the famine, but we did live.

There is a holly of him in the block data bank, taken when he enlisted. It holds the head and shoulders of a round-faced boy, with lank mousecoloured hair, eyes front and features composed for posterity. There is little to learn from the image: he doesn't seem enigmatic or eager or indifferent. It is just a boy's head put into the records. I can see that it could be William Coombes, although the most characteristic thing about it is the impression it leaves of anonymity: any number of men might have looked like that when they were boys. Only if you look at the boy's eyes you see that they are pale and colourless: not blue but a washed-out yellow brown, at that moment focussed on nothing and seeming to have neither surface nor depth. They give a distinction to the boy's face which I never saw in Mr. Coombes', since one avoids the eyes of a living man. Unless you already knew that he was a mad plant manager, you would hardly have noticed Mr. Coombes.

I first met him when he started to walk home from the plant. That would be about two years after he came home. He had to report at the block office when he came in, and as he generally came in about twenty, and I had the evening shift, he usually reported to me. I was uneasy with him at first: this part of the world was badly hit during the Atlantic War – we are only fifty kilometres from Crater – and even now there is a general shelter order in force because of the radiation levels. Eighteen years ago the radiation levels were higher, the sick areas had only recently been closed, 'clean' air was even dirtier than it is now, and very few people went onto the roofs, let alone into the lanes. Mr. Coombes had asked permission to walk home regularly from the plant. To do it he would have to start by climbing through the highway, which was dangerous in itself, then make a long detour round Bryant, which is closed. He couldn't hope to make the journey in much less than three hours: most of them spent below roof level.

It is easy to say now that he was sixty-four years old last year and still working, when most of his age, certainly most veterans, were dead. Without hindsight it seemed suicidal: a frightening sign of weakness in a useful citizen. And when permission was refused he went to the panel and got a medical clearance on therapeutic grounds.

It is unnerving when a man directly responsible for the food supply to half a million people is given such a lethal therapy. It suggests terrible disease; more terribly it suggests a diseased mind. But the world doesn't foster serenity, and we put up with each others' twitches when we can. When the food still came it was easy to shut one's eyes to the walks. And Mr. Coombes was quite controlled; he had even married, although his wife was a shorthaul pilot so they weren't together too much. His wife was young then, but they had no children.

For nearly twenty years of careful routine he lived in the same two rooms on this block. The routine was enlivened daily by the climb across the highway, and threatened by signs of age, but the only erratic element in it was the presence of his wife, who came and went according to uncertain schedules, and for whom his feelings must at least have been ambiguous. I won't say that he seemed content, but at least he did not seem distressed. He functioned efficiently.

He disappeared last autumn when he was walking home one evening. People do disappear: quite a number according to the civil guard. Probably most of them just leave and join the migrant work pool. Maybe a few manage to forge identity seals and merge back into the State. Some must be dead: accidentally obliterated in a block clearance perhaps, or washed away in the gulley. People suicide in the gulleys, everyone knows, and their bodies are filtered out and identified and rendered down; but they don't find them all.

I think Mr. Coombes had too much sense to join the pool at his age, and he was certainly too scrupulous to forge a seal. I don't think he killed himself either, and I know he would never have chosen to die in a gulley.

I worry about him. There is no sensible reason to suppose that anything unusual happened to him; it is only unusual that he survived the walks for so long. He probably just died and was tidied away by a servitor. We sent out a couple of search parties who found nothing, and after three months there was a memorial meeting, and his wife filed for insurance and was moved away to a room at the port. Mr. Coombes' deputy took over at the plant, and although we haven't had a sweet ration for six months we are eating quite well.

I worry about him I suppose because of the landing last spring. He was the main witness: the only witness who got a close look, and it left him disturbed and unlike himself. During the summer he was excitable, sullen, almost garrulous. He would sometimes interrupt quite different discussions to talk about the landing, and we prepared to pull in our belts. I may have given the impression that he did talk a lot about himself, but you must remember that I knew him for a long time. I picked up a lot of his history from odd references and by inference, but I might have seen the landing myself: he told us so often what he did, what he saw, what he felt.

At seventeen thirty one on the day of the landing he was in the highway, half-way up a ten metre ladder which connected a surviving section of pedestrian way with a makeshift catwalk. His feet were bare, because it gave him an illusion of safety to know that he could grip with toes and fingers as he climbed, and the sandals stuffed in the pocket of his coat swung as he moved and bumped against his shins. He knew it was seventeen thirty one because the rusty metal under his hand began to vibrate slightly, and a chip of concrete worked loose from the pillar he was climbing, bounced on a girder, and dropped away below. He thought if he hurried he might reach the catwalk before the super came over, but after a few rungs dust began to pour down the face of the pillar and he decided to hang on where he was. He clasped the ladder, half shut his eyes, and listened to the wheeze of a transport bedding down for the blow. He saw the whole pillar shake and then a slam of sound plucked at him and the ladder or the pillar moved. He could feel the grind of staples pulling from their mounts, but before he had time to be afraid the sound ebbed to a roar of wind and the wind died, and he could hear the transport again heaving off its rail. It started to move, scraped its rail with a wild screech, stopped, gasped, and heaved again, then swung past him in a cloud of dust. He could see people through the sealed windows all crushed indifferently together: talking quite happily or peering out at the highway, and instead of emphasizing his own freedom the sight seemed to enfold him. Friends near the windows recognized him and waved and cheered: he could see their mouths open wide then slowly close, their hands slap the glass above their heads, drawing him to them. He closed his eyes and when he opened them the transport had gone. He started to climb again, very carefully because the ladder shifted every time he moved.

The catwalk was very beautiful: a sliver of translucent crystal clipped at one end to the ladder head and at the other, fifteen metres away, to the parapet of a bombed underpass. It was SPEC surplus: used because it was available and the right length, and one of its characteristics was a low friction surface. A metal handrail had been fixed to one side of it, but over the years two crewmen had slipped and fallen, so later a length of cable had been slung across above head height.

Mr. Coombes reached up for the cable with both hands and side-stepped towards the distant parapet with careful poise, balancing his weight above the board. He had no faith in his ability to haul himself to safety by hand if he lost his foothold. Some way above him were the speed rails and below him was a long drop to ground level. Several days of high winds had cleared the air, and although he could not see the ground road he could just discern the dark line of the Northampton gulley. Set between the high rails and the gulley, and bounded by the plant to the west and Southern Diversified to the east, were the Midlands throughways and the through rail, local roads and rails, the plant sidings and loading bays, and all the shunts and crossovers of the Bedford intersection. Embedded in the web were the ruins of abandoned systems: bombed flyovers and obsolete tube lines crumbled away, rotten but entrenched. They were shored up by scaffolding and site cast casings, and in turn they shored up systems still in use, but hardly less dilapidated.

The highway is all metal and concrete and simple plastics; only the speed rails use organics and they should be quite separate. There are two threads running from south to north and north to south, high above the whole mess. Their struts are rooted in the earth, which should take the full shock of the supers and leave the highway undisturbed; but at Hockliff the struts have grown into parts of the highway, to strengthen it, so when a super comes over everything trembles.

He had crossed daily for years, and because nothing ever

quite collapsed he usually ignored the signals of decay. But sometimes on the catwalk, where he was most aware of his vulnerability, he saw danger and was afraid. He saw it as he looked down at the gulley, and stood with his eyes closed to gather courage. He had opened his eyes and was about to move again when he felt himself fall. He still clutched the cable above his head and his toes still clenched on the crystal board, but he knew he was falling and the high rails above him were falling too. Everything was toppling soundlessly inwards so slowly that he could see no movement, and he said those words in his mind: there is no movement, there is no movement; knowing that the words were true, but not believing them.

Perhaps he would have fallen if the vertigo had lasted for more than a few seconds, but it passed and he was left clinging to his perch with everything as it had been. A mist of rain eddied round him.

When he had crossed the rest of the catwalk and reached the remains of the Bryant underpass he walked out to what had been the middle of the middle lane; eased himself down; and sat there on the roadway for a while, listening to the cars on the road above and the juggers far below: comforted for once because they were customary sounds.

He had no fear of heights. After a while he climbed carefully down to ground level, but his caution was deliberate. His impulse was to let go, to float, to fall. He had schooled himself to accept stiff joints and unresponsive muscles and failing judgment, but had counted on warning signals. Now all his senses together had slipped out of his control and might go again and it was too abrupt. By the time he reached the ground he was shaking and didn't know whether it was shock or some fresh sign of disintegration.

He found a cat in the storm drain under the Bedford ground level filter. But now it was dark, and as always the drain was filled with the shaking roar of juggers on the filter road. It was a big drain-more like a tunnel, but he had to crouch over as he walked through it, and as he reached the outlet his hand brushed against fur and his bare foot kicked involuntarily and pushed something live into the diffuse light of the passing traffic. The animal sprawled loosely where he had kicked it, lying as if it was drugged, but when he touched it gently with his toe it winced and scrabbled aimlessly for a moment against the rough concrete, then lay still again.

He took his sandals out of his pocket and dropped them to the ground, then shuffled them on to his feet without bending. He touched the cat again with the edge of his sandal, but this time it hardly moved. He knelt down reluctantly, and lifted it gently into his arms. It lay with its eyes slightly open: a small plump animal with torn ears. It looked wrong, almost boneless. He thought it was dying.

It was difficult to get up again with both hands occupied, and he almost put the cat down again and abandoned it. But he was ashamed to leave it there to die. He held it with one arm, pushed against the damp wall of the drain with the other, and managed to stagger to his feet. He could take it over to the guardpost at Diversified and leave it with them.

He crawled back through the drain and went along the bank of the filter, looking for a gap in the Diversified fence. The bank was in shadow, only dimly lit by the lights of the ground filter reflected from the higher roads. The evening air was still quite clear though, and he could see the teeth along the top of the ten metre fence.

He was stopped by the hulk of a jugger, which had run off the road and done its best to climb the fence. The forward unit was draped over the sagging mesh, nose up as if it was trying to take off. The rear unit was actually balanced vertically behind it, nose down in the ditch, and he saw as he came closer that the end left on the road had simply been lifted clear with a couple of cables hitched to an overhead gantry. One part of the twisted fence had lifted away from its moorings and he stepped under it and round the heavy shadow of the suspended transport into the compound.

He had seen a service tunnel which should take him towards the guardpost, and he went back and walked through it by the light of a roadcleaner which rattled along behind him too slowly to be much of a danger. The servitor turned away down a side tunnel just as he emerged into a cleared site, and he was left quite suddenly in silence looking across the great canyon of bared earth confined by high blank walls.

It was quite unexpected. The canyon stretched away ahead of him so far that he could not see the far wall, and was hundreds of metres wide – almost as wide as its walls were high. He realized that the huge servitor parked in the corner nearest to him was a recycling unit: he had come across a block clearance in the few hours between dissolving and moulding. There were lights behind him in the mouth of the tunnel, and a roadway dewed with rain led out across the open space towards a vague glow of light which must be the same tunnel continuing. The rest of the vast plain was mud and stones. He could imagine it lapping the sealed walls.

The earth was only an infill of course. There was a stamp of half-dissolved plastic pushing from the soil at his feet, which must be a load point founded on a deep shelter platform. The deep shelter would spread under the soil just as the blocks spread above it. Still, the soil was real. He walked forward along the roadway into the darkness and stood there entranced, still holding the damaged animal unthinkingly.

There was a sound.

A short way away below the road another fragment of pillar had been left upright, and in its shadow something with a thin high voice was saying, or singing, 'La-la-la-la-la-la-la-la-la-' on one note, quietly.

'La-la-la-la-la-la-la.' Silence.

'L-l-l-l-lll.' A squeak. Silence.

'Hhhhaaaaaaa ... Hhhhhhaaaaa ... Hhhhhhhaaa.' Silence. Hallo?

'Hallo?' said Mr. Coombes.

'Nnnnnnnnn. Nnnnnnnn.'

'Hallo?'

'Nnn-Nnn-Nn.' No?

He scrambled down from the roadway onto the black earth and walked towards the stump of pillar.

'Rrrrrrrrrrrrrrrrrrrrr' trilled the voice sweetly. Perhaps it was alarmed. Perhaps it was growling. Perhaps it did not know he was there. He stopped and peered into the dark. He could just see the uneven ground where he stood, and the edge of the wet road behind him showed as a line of light, but below the stump was black dark, and the source of the voice was engulfed.

'Hhhhaa . . . Hhhha . . .' breathed the voice, and in concert the cat breathed: air shrilled in its throat and its ribs juddered under his thumb. He touched it helplessly, willing it to die.

It seemed to him as he stood that the dark became less dark, and then that it stayed black but was flecked with transitory points of light. And then it was black again for a moment, and then a single white flare expanded within reach of his fingers, died, flared again, and drifted away to the pillar. He followed it. Far away someone shouted and shouted again. He heard the shouts and their echoes, then a shouted reply and its echo and its echo; then a sector bell began to ring insistently, hardly audible at this distance. He heard the sounds and echoes of alarm, but he listened to the small voice, which went 'Sssssssss . . . Sssssssssss' with the tiny sibilance of a whisper, and he looked at what he had supposed was a load point, where the white light shone on rock. Not on plastic but on creature rock, veined with green.

The voice said 'Vul. Vul. Vul!' With emphatic precision.

Afterwards his memory of the incident was flawed, and for at least a week he insisted that everything had happened on the plant roof, before he had left for home. He rebuilt his memory about the clear image of black flaking rock: faceted and glinting in the strange light, and about the unexpected feel of it when he reached out and nervously caressed it: that it was not smooth but gritty, even as it shone.

There is no clear account of what happened next. The group of guards who raised the alarm were too far away to see more than a suggestion of light. There had been radio interference on their spyviews, and its source was at least in the direction of the light, which faded away while they were still gathering at the far tunnel entrance. When they reached Mr. Coombes he was lying unconscious in the mud. They scanned the area before they carried him away to the post, but saw nothing notable. When they were questioned later they were reasonably certain that there had been no rock, no load point, no animal in the area.

Mr. Coombes was only certain of the rock. He could remember touching its solid crumbling surface, and he could remember believing that the cat was dead. By then he could only see light without definition, which pervaded everything. His own body seemed to have vanished into light. The cat's tortured breathing had eased and he could feel it lying soft and relaxed in his arm, and then he just felt that it was dead. There was no obvious change: only the sense of dead weight. Even if his memory of the moment was sound he could only remember an impression, and soon after that he lost all sensation: even the light became indistinguishable from dark and his hands touched nothing and he stood on nothing and did not know whether what he heard was silence or some unrecognizable blaze of sound.

The first aid kit at the guardpost malfunctioned and soaked him in Destroy, which woke him up, but he was confused and only remembered slowly and imperfectly. SPEC set up a big investigation and held up the recycling for three days while they ran every sort of test on the site and found nothing. People as far away as Crater claimed that they had felt a moment of dizziness at about seventeen-thirty, and five civil guards agreed that there was some kind of light on the site, but there was only Mr. Coombes' account for the rest.

Most people believed him, and I think SPEC was still interested, but his story had no pattern to it, and no place in the patterns of our experience. Interest faded, and it has probably been filed away with all the other trivia like cahias and ESP: things which may well occur, but which cannot be codified and exploited.

He remembered the final message of the voice in a dream, months later – long after he had pieced together the other fragments. 'He was dreaming of something else when the voice said 'Vul parahannis' very clearly and fluently in its small monotone, and he woke up. He believed then that he remembered it, but he may only have remembered an earlier dream.

That's all really. As I say he was disturbed for a few months, but even that was less obvious after a while. He rang through one evening in November to say that he was just leaving the plant. I took the call myself and said 'Thank you', and 'I'll see you later then', or some other obvious remark, and there was nothing at all in his voice or his words to distinguish that call from the ones he had made every evening for years. He didn't come in, and at twenty-two I raised the alarm as a precaution: thinking that he had been delayed at the plant. At four we sent out a small search party to follow his route, and later that day there was a big sweep with as many volunteers as they could get from the pool and a lot of personnel servitors. People were very anxious and several citizens wanted to help; so they were issued with masks and deployed in the block lanes, where Mrs. Rhiak fell off a monorail and broke a wrist. There was no trace at all of Mr. Coombes.

To me there is a pattern in what I've told you, and of all its parts it is the cat which worries me most. Mr. Coombes was certain that the cat died, and I'm sure he came to believe that if it was not there the voice must have taken it. But I believe myelf that it had been paralysed, then galvanized, by terror; and had simply run away: so that it should be the most ordinary element in the pattern: far more natural for instance than Rachel Kwe escaping from Earth to a glass bowl, and more credible than alien voices in the Midlands. But all those other things are just events. Very unusual events it is true, but Mr. Coombes had had an unusual life, and things which seemed to me unbelievable were a commonplace to him.

It is easy to explain the disappearance of the cat. What worries me; or at least undermines my reasoning with bad dreams, is that it completes a neat array of symbols. I think that for Mr. Coombes cats were a talisman of true survival. We survive too, but he saw the last small birds of his childhood die in the air, and the other free animals of his maturity: rats and people; scutter fearfully to the safe cages of their blocks and gullies, while cats still prowl down plastic corridors as if they were in living jungle. In the summertime they go on the roofs and stretch out in the sun: dozing on their backs like babies with their paws in the air, or they chase paper blown by the wind. In winter they sit by the heat vents and wash themselves and snap at the small insects blown up through the ducts, or they hunt through the service levels and eat the insects there. A cat lying with its eyes closed for hours in the sun might as well be anywhere at any time, and cats stalking mice through long grass a hundred years ago cannot have been more absorbed than our cats stalking cockroaches among the drying frames.

Mr. Coombes made himself stand easily in crowded cubicles and accept greetings and handclasps with a smile; and would see through the bars some underfed cat washing itself with its eyes closed, and he would envy it.

Now Mr. Coombes came to believe that the dead cat had gone through a door which he might pass alive. His only evidence was his own need and I believe none of it, and yet since he disappeared I worry. I know it is nonsense but I connect Rachel Kwe and the cat and Mr. Coombes and I imagine that the voice came again. Of course it didn't because there was no vertigo, but I imagine that it came again and that William Coombes walked into it. He had always been obsessed with the possibility of escape, but I don't think of him as escaping. He had already seen the only escape, in acceptance: there can be nowhere else to go that would have any meaning for a man.

I remember that when he found the cat he could not bring himself to leave it alone to die.

He was so bound to Earth that when he thought of escape he thought of translation to some other, empty, Earth. But suppose one escaped to something one could not sense, or could sense but not interpret: to be trapped in one's own skin, or darkness or infinity or the little broken gyro of one's own unoriented mind?

We have a song here which fits to the tune of *Vostock Ferry*. Its chorus goes 'No one to share my bath, No one to share my bath, We're five to a bed but that's all I ask, No one to share my bath.'

Probably he just died.

THE WAY ERVING WENT

by

GRAHAME LEMAN

Here is a forceful and demotic example of the old saw that there are more outside than in. Grahame Leman, who last appeared in New Writings in SF volume 23, points up sharply the proposition that comedy strikes more directly to the vital heart of our human affairs than ever tragedy can, especially if your buddy goes blue and whump, into the bargain.

THE WAY ERVING WENT

Erving has disappeared, and I don't think I can stand it in this bin without Erving. It's not just that he *has* disappeared, and so isn't here: it's the *way* he went. Well, let's take it from the beginning:

If it's a rest you're wanting, some respite from the *Sturm und Drang* of life in these Americas at the dirty end of the twentieth century, don't you make the (my!) big mistake of acting crazy to get yourself put away in the bin. All right, I do know the only way to get into a hospital at all these days – unless you're a millionaire, have the kind of job that carries Gold Cross with it, or are dying with useful spare parts to spare – is to act too crazy to be safe on the street and get yourself certified and binned. But believe one who's tried it: you're two three times better off on the outside, sweating twelve hours a day to keep up with the cybersystem, sleeping five to a room, spending five hours of the rest of the day processing pollutants out of tapwater, and trying to believe the food the government says is safe *is* safe; even if you had a fine friend like Erving inside with you. *Much* better off.

Since the taxpayer stopped taxpaying for exponential annual increase in research funds, cost-benefit analysis has hit science some blows, and research has to pay or else; while the population explosion and the soaring incidence of pollution-induced disease had finished Medicare before it hardly began, and patients have to pay their way in some kind of coin.

This bin (a half-heartedly converted military camp down in NJ) lives by doing cut-price contract research for European and Third World countries and corporations, and they keep the prices down by getting plenty of mileage out of the experimental preparations (that is, the people here apart

31

from the staff). Professor Oehler is using me to find out whether or not shock treatment will suppress artificial psychoses induced by lysergic acid derivatives; Doctor (of philosophy, psychopharmacologist) Trice is trying to see if he can develop a non-addictive major analgesic before he kills me; I have been pressed into some Australian researcher's somatic group therapy trials; and Doctor (medic, specializing sexology) Myra Feuerbach is trying to induce functional impotence in me by crash hypnosis, in aid of the population problem. It's all voluntary, of course: they have to ask you to sign their piece of paper, and if you won't sign they can't touch you, the government is very hot on that; but after they've given you the crash course of spider 98, the complex of huts where they keep the people who don't volunteer and attract a diagnosis of antisocial tendencies, most of us do volunteer; even Erving volunteered.

What with the post-shock amnesias, the acid fugues, the painful withdrawals from addictions to Trice's unlucky shots, the violence in the somatic group therapy (only last week I won a black eye and two cracked ribs fending off a butch ex-teamster who had been shot full of barb and told to act out his philithy phantasies), and of course the sexual obsessions implanted in me by fire-eyes Feuerbach's graunched hypnoses, it's a wonder I can manage to keep the ward clean and do the laundry and the dishes (that's my occupational therapy, for reality-testing and to keep my manual dexterities in fine tune).

Doctor Ellen (sour redhead from Seattle, psychiatric intern) Born, who supervises the symbolic group therapy, didn't love Erving: like me, only much more so, Erving was bright, well and curiously read, been around, and he could put pickled Born down in argument without straining; which made her tell him (in spite of the fact that *her* idea of a warm human response was, notoriously, a smouldering fit of the sulks) that paranoiacs are all alike, they can make any kind of cold sense but no kind of warm sense – which was why Erving was a mere preparation while *she* was a quack.

Erving had gotten into this bin here by pestering the FBI, the air force, the space force, sundry congressmen, anybody who would stand still for it: telling them he was a Martian investigator, come to discover why the surface of Ølorn appeared so diseased from a great distance, and that we Ølornians must do what he (Erving) said – before we wiped ourselves out in some ecocrash. Well, as they told him, more than a dozen sensible men have *been* to Mars to see (keeping their hair short and changing their underpants daily: all the way thither, there, and back again), and we just *know*, like scientifically, that there's no life on Mars at all like Erving: which makes Erving a nut, grade A; especially as he kept insisting he was the only (inconsistently) *man* alive who knew how to save us from an early and irremediable disaster – because people who see themselves like that *do* very often kill people without warning, for reasons that don't make any consensually valid kind of sense to the consensus.

It didn't bother Erving when Born, one of the other quacks, or one of his enemies among the patients threw the no-life-on-Mars objection at him: of *course* there's no Erving-like life on Mars *now*, he used to say, because the true Martians had made a few itsy mistakes with the Martial ecosystem and had had to move off, most of them to some other star a few years off; but a few to what Erving *would* call Ølorn (pronounced 'fer-lawn', and supposed to be the name of our Earth in the Old High Martial tongue), where they degenerated in a few centuries into henge-builders, metaphysicians, cave-painters, prophets, Homeridae, geometers, and primitive rabble of that kind. Hadn't we ever wondered, he used to ask, why he from Mars was just plain what we call human on Ølorn?: well, *that* was why, it was obvious once you knew the history.

Now, I just don't have the brains Erving had (you know how it is, I can app*reci*ate a thought once someone else has thought it, no matter *how* far out, but I can't think such thoughts myself): I could never have gotten myself into the bin by thinking up a ramified, rebuttal-proof (you should have *heard* his refutations of refutations of his claims) delusional system like Erving's lovely messiah-from-Mars routine.

What I did, I just tried to tell everybody the plain truth all the time: I had discovered as a child that people think you are at least mad and probably bad, too, if you do that. For instance, I used to teach my students at Columbia (till they fired me) that there is no such thing as knowledge, nothing can be *known*, and what passes for scientific knowledge is just the current fashion in preconceptions and about as durable as this season's skirt length or keynote colour; and I still tell the quacks here the same thing: if I was comfortably dead like Hume or Kant, they might cite me in the jargonized papers and reports they keep endlessly writing; as I'm uncomfortably alive, they write me down in the case file as dysfunctionally out of touch with consensually valid reality, and wonder aloud *where I can hear them* about the possibility of curing scepticism by surgical intervention (cutting things out of my head or implanting things in it). But what got me in here, I guess, was my campaign insisting that we would have to do a crash cull of nine in ten of the people on Earth, to avoid a more toxic ecocrash (including myself, as a philosopher with none of the skills, such as horsemanship, that would be needed in a de-industrialized world): well, *you* know who my father is – I am too important to laugh off or put in jail, but there is no harm in saying I am mad and disregarding my simple arithmetic on that count.

Nobody, least of all the Born, believed that the symbolic group therapy would do anybody any good, bar providing well-paid work for Born and passing the time for the preparations (sorry, patients): *she* didn't think she would change the minds of people who were all either more intelligent or tougher characters than she was, and *we* didn't think we would succumb to the going theodicy and become reconciled to life, either in here or out there. The Born used to treat the sessions as pure entertainment: cabaret, circus with clowns for the kiddies, Roman circus with Christians for the grown-ups, carny with monsters; like the boxing in prisons, this got quite a reputation as a free show, and we used to have to put up with visiting researchers, medics, politicos, and sundry girl friends from all over the state and even from the big cities.

The star turn was the Born trying to knock down Erving's ramified messiah-from-Mars routine: she spent a lot of her spare time browsing about in the xenological literature about life on other bodies in the solar system, and she used to pitch Erving some real wild screw balls.

For instance, she used to say that diggers on Mars had found nothing in the Martial strata to suggest an evolution of even large living things with rudimentary brains, so how did Erving account for the existence of 'true Martians'?: and Erving used to say, the trouble with *her* idea of evolution was that it was just too parochial, both in space and in time; that people evolved in the *universe*, not on planets – which explained the puzzling discontinuity in the fossil records, discreditably neglected by the blinkered evolutionists of Ølorn. Or she would ask why, if there had been true Martians all along, they had never come to call before?: and Erving just said they did in earlier times, having dropped in now and again to remind the degenerate plantations of the uses of fire, to do the consulting mathematical astronomy for sundry henge-builders, and anything else that seemed useful when they happened to be passing and looked in; but, after one of their ships blew up and left a whole crew stranded in the part of Ølorn we call Greece, they didn't risk landing for many centuries. So why didn't they come *now* more often, the Born would go on, now that we were signalling our proliferation by radiating television Westerns, newsak, old movies, *rel*evant documentaries, and late night yak shows to the neighbouring stars?: and Erving would say, did *she* visit pestiferous slums precisely because she read in her paper how pestiferous they were, or didn't she roll up the window of the cab going thru Harlem?

The only way the Born could cheat a win in these gladiations, was to turn after a while to one of the distinguished visitors and tell them to notice the characteristic hermetic elaboration of a full-blown delusional system, prognosis lousy.

Erving used to cheer me up, when I felt black guilty and blue low about copping out of the struggle for negative growth and escaping in here, where nobody will expect me to know what to do next about the pullulating population, the pollution, the shortages, and the politicians' daily ritual speeches exalting Growth as the answer to all these 'transient' problems.

'Suppose', Erving would say, 'Ølorn *is* destroyed in some ecocrash – well, so what?: surely, that would be better than things going on as they go only more so? Don't forget what all your scientists say, that there must be hundreds of millions of planets in the universe bearing intelligent life: so whatever happens here is about as important as one bacterium in a culture dying a little sooner instead of living a little longer; a wrong evolutionary move will be cancelling itself, that's all. What you have here on Ølorn is a comedy of presumption, not some grand hubristic Tragedy.'

Tragedy or comedy?; comedy or Tragedy?: that's what I keep thinking now. Now: since last night: when Erving disappeared.

The Born once brought a friend of hers down from New York City to lecture us on the dramatic genres ('So you're all role-players, you bums; it follows you should get some of those *deep* insights from Buck's inside view of the drammer, right?'): a high-yaller Jewish television writer, with a funny right half to his face – the alcoholic adman who spawned him used to knock him about in the cradle (once too hard) when he cried at night. According to him, Tragedy is sentimental, deceiving: a way of slopping a sugar coat of such goodies as glory, destiny, dignity, whataveyou on things like defeat and death, that should be taken straight; whereas comedy is clear-eyed, informative: shows you stupid mistakes you don't *have* to make for yourself to convince yourself.

'Mind you', I remember him saying, 'You might want to take a good look at me and discount my line. Just try to imagine *me* shaving in front of the bathroom mirror, then sitting down at the typewriter to knock together some glory and dignity to wear around.

As I was saying, Erving went last night. While I was polishing the brass in the topstaff john, Erving sneaked in and hauled me off to the furnace room for a quiet talk. There were some makings behind our ward's own loose brick, back of the boiler, and I rolled a fat joint for us to share; but get this straight, I'm *used* to the stuff, and it was weak weed anyway, cut to Hell; so there's no need to think I wasn't clear-headed. After some chit-chat about the deliberate starvation policy of the new Indian government, Erving made me wedge the bench between the front of the boiler and the only door to the furnace room, and sit on it so we wouldn't be discovered.

'Frank', he said: 'I got to say so long. More like good-bye. Thing is, I'm leaving Ølorn tonight – for good, I guess.'

'What you *mean*, you're leaving here, Erving? You leave here, about fifteen-point-five current experiments going to get screwed up to nothing – and three quacks are going to lose grant renewal. How you think you're going to get *out* of here Erving? Are the Black Panthers coming for you with a regiment of armour or something.

'Well, I *got* to be leaving, Frank. Listen, did you see the Sunday supplements in the television lounge yesterday? Did you see how the scientists say they have discovered a USO – that is, Unprecedented Stellar Object, around the co-ordinates of Vega in the Lyre? Did you see how the Russians on the moon have accused Italian photographers of making unauthorized pictures of the private lives of their crews up there? Well, Frank, that wasn't no stellar object; and it wasn't no Italian paparazzi with long lenses: *that* was my wife come for me.'

I just looked at him. What can you say? And, anyway, I didn't want him to stop. Which he didn't:

'She's the ... Captain, you would say, of a space-time survey ship. She happened to be cruising along a world-line that intersects with Ølorn's world-line, and sector headquarters told her to pick me up. Apparently they want me to mend something or other not far from Rigel. That's my trade, mending things – when they're not past saving. So, I have to say good-bye, Frank.'

'But how're you going to get *out*, Erving?'

'Oh, that'll be easy enough. The wife's ship has a thing we call a Lazy Beam, for picking things up and putting them somewhere else. She'll use that. It's just a matter of picking up the bit of 3-space my body occupies, moving it into 4-space, and putting it back into 3-space again inside her ship. You know, Frank: like, if you were a flat-lander, shut up inside a 2-space circle, you'd think you couldn't get out; but solidlanders living in ordinary 3-space can see that you could be lifted out of 2-space into 3-space, then put back in 2-space *outside* the circle; from the flatland standpoint, you'd vanish from inside the circle and appear again outside. Well, it's like that, only more so.'

'You'll vanish? Whomp!, just like that?'

'Sure.'

'But someone will see you! Wouldn't that do us harm here on Earth, on Ølorn? Like the Born says in the bull-sessions, if you were a real Martian, you wouldn't come here and mess around: in case we Earthians get culture-shock or something. Should a decent Martian *do* a thing like that, Erving?'

'Who's to see? Seems to me we've made ourselves pretty nice and private here in the furnace room. Nice and private.'

'Me! *I'll* see you vanish into 4-space. Whomp!'

'Well, that's all right. Nobody'll believe you, if you tell. Why, Frank, you're certified psychotic, not fit to be on the street; you don't even believe in J. Edgar, the American Medical Association, and Growth, do you? Why would anybody who *is* anybody listen to a psychotic bum like you? No problem.'

'Anyway, Erving, I wouldn't tell. Thing is, I don't believe you. For one thing, I don't believe people go *whomp*; for another, I don't believe you *are* a descendant of the old Martians, from outer space. That's just your malinger, to get in here: where you thought it would be better than outside, trying to keep ahead of the cybersystem.'

'Now look, Frank! You remember telling me how you got into this bin?: by telling the plain truth loud and clear. Well, so did I. Notoriously, it's the best way to get certified crazy and put in the bin, isn't it?'

'So prove you're a Martian, Erving!'

There was a crackle, a smell of electricity in the air. Sparking in the blower motor of the furnace, or something. Erving nodded, as if he had been expecting it, and began to strip; went on till he was mother naked. He put both hands on my shoulders and looked right in my eyes, making me feel funny. He refused another pull on the weed, too.

'Frank', he said: 'I could prove it a hundred ways. Why, I could give you the algorithm for a two-minute slide-rule solution of the three-body problem, or a demonstrative proof of Fermat's last theorem – even a simple formula for a cure for the common cold. But what I *am* going to do, very soon, is: *one* turn blue and sort of transparent; *two* go very faint so you can hardly see me; *three* go whomp! When you see me go blue, Frank, you got to get right off behind the boiler, plug both ears with your index fingers, hold your nostrils closed with your little fingers, and keep your mouth tight shut: when I go whomp, as much air as me will rush into the place where I was – and, in this little room, you'll be hit by something like a wave of explosive decompression. But do what I say, and you'll take no harm.'

Damned if Erving didn't start turning blue, too. Well, there was something *about* Erving – he had *authority;* even if you didn't believe him, you naturally tended to jump when he said jump. So I got behind the boiler and did the other things he said. There was a whomp all right (maybe more like a whump, really: it didn't *hit*, it *pulled*), and I think I passed out for a couple of seconds. When I came round, Erving was gone, nothing but his clothes tumbled over in a corner. So I got the bench out of the way, opened the door, shut it again from the outside; and sneaked back to the topstaff john and my polishing, in case I got involved in any kind of investigation or inquiry. I certainly saw Erving turn blue, and I never saw him again.

Well, Senator, you see how it is. I'm sorry it had to be written on a roll of toilet paper, like an ancient manuscript (lucky they don't perforate this official issue paper); and I'm sorry the shift key is missing from the typewriter I liberated from an ashcan back of the office block (if you ask *me*, e. e. cummings was twee). But it's all clear enough, I'm sure. You may be a big wheel now, Senator, but you'll remember the time my old man got those blackmailers off your neck, after you'd mortgaged your home to buy television time on your first run for Mayor?: anyway, *I* remember it, Senator. So you got to get me out of here.

Maybe you could tell my old man, I realize now it takes two to make a real break, him and me both; and I'll come half-way back to meet him, if he'll come the other half-way back. Last time I heard of him he was trying to find a face-saving solution to the hundred-year Warm War in Asia. You can see I need his help. And *your* help, Senator, and your help: happy days, that Tijuana hooker you were photographed with in the motel that night was really built for it, wasn't she?; and the pot of money you made helping her brother get 'pharmaceuticals' across the border was a real, ten ton, end-of-the-rainbow honeycrock of sweet gold, wasn't it, Senator? So get me *out* of here! You hear?

What it is: if this is all a tragedy, then I've got it made already. You know, there are a few intelligent people who know the score sitting here and there in places like this, while all the madmen outside the walls are wrecking the world. It's a poetically satisfying picture, definitely: there's destiny for you, there's dignity for you – or rather for me.

But if it's just a *comedy*! Dammit, Erving *did* turn blue and sort of transparent; and where is he now?; can J. Edgar and the chastity boys find Erving? If it's just a *comedy*, if the end of the world is just a wry little moral (like the don't-can-your-man-this-week-honey-they're-all-like-that resolution in the tag-end of a Lucy show) that'll teach other races between the stars an itsy lesson (there but for the grace of the Demiurge goes *our* collective foot on the great banana skin; hearty laughter; switch off the damn commercials, Øanni)

... Well, are we going to put up with *that*? Is it our Manifest Destiny to educate the popcorn (whompcorn?, øoøkernels?) chewers of the local group of galaxies, by doing a lethal pratfall just before the last commercial break?

No! The sane people had better get out of the madhouses and try to see that the world doesn't go whomp, whump, or whimper, to nothing. You'll be my first recruit and frontman, Senator. No, wait: admittedly, you've *got* to do it, because I happen to know all about that business down on the border near Tijuana. But it isn't going to be as bad as that: you might be able to run for President on this line (like Mackie, Misky, Michie ... whatever his name was, way back).

One way and another, Senator, I don't think I can stand it in here any longer, doing nothing about things I ought to be doing something about. Especially now Erving is gone. It's the way he went. If you don't get me *out* of here, Senator, I think I shall go *crazy*.

THE BANKS OF THE NILE

by

Ritchie Smith *and* Thomas Penman

Against a baroque and densely textured patterning of cultural fragments, vivid and evocative, Emmanuel Kyygard bestrides a treacherous and blood-soaked age. Here the shadows of Renaissance and Reformation, Machiavelli and Borgia, and dark future centuries of violence infested by the tang and bite of the black light of decadent science, interact to touch a nerve. Ritchie Smith and Thomas Penman present their depiction of a vision of the future rich in betrayal and glittering with menace. A future in which the iron demands of Empire draw forth a more dreadful resolution than any mere staining of the map of Europa with blood.

THE BANKS OF THE NILE

HUNG UP in a wind, cradled under the silver-fish hundred and sixty yards of our zeppelin, we fell across the countryside.

Boreas, the North Wind, had met us over the Vosges: it was late summer there. Or early autumn perhaps, the coming on of the season of mists and mellow fruitlessness. Below us the French wheatfields' richness had spread yellow-bronze friezes of a peculiar washed out hue; but now, with the flesh of Europe still passing beneath us, there appeared the seas of blood-red poppies of Flanders. Each one is a bloody grave-mark: a place, but no name, no date . . . Passchendaele, the Somme . . . A hurting-time in the elder world, but long centuries ease those recollected pains.

And yet the rustle of the wind in our dirigible's struts, as I stood in the bows, might have been the faint whispering of the dead resting still beneath the crimson plains. To the southwest lie the beaches of England's Normandy, another graveyard from another war. Southward is Versailles, and the Isle de France.

The past is too much with us. I turned my head out of the wind and spat; it was a long way for my blessing to fall.

The powersong of our steam-jet ducted fans throbbed anew, deepened, as I guided us high above the sunny pewter of the Channel, and paused to smile with an ironic benevolence at the shipping there. Across the straits rose Dover's white-washed cliff fangs, bared powerless now: soon we sailed above their reach, into the Empire of Albion. There, where old Father Thames wound through the ringwalls of Londres eastward to the sea, waited Charles IX of England. Son of the last occupant of the Iron Throne, Empress Elizabeth, and, so rumour whispers, the greatest and most exotically flamboyant of her generals.

'Emmanuel Kyygard . . .' Annah said, and I focussed on

her, on her arched brows; she was basking in a tepid blaze of sun that cobwebbed her black satin catsuit and glistened on her tooled and embroidered boots of Spanish leather, 'high emissary of the King . . .' She half knelt and slid a black, iron-wood hilted blade from its sheath beside my calf, 'lover . . .' her naked, willowy white arm lightly caressing the rib-like weaving of aluminium over our heads, 'if you are knighted for this work, will you remember me . . .?'

The north-needle swung away as I over-compensated for Boreas' wicked autumn breath, then settled. I unhooked both elevator bars from their ratchet-stops and hauled on them, the wind-strummed control cables creaking metal-lically as they passed on the pull to the great fins at the stern. I looked out in exhilaration, as we soared, amidst scudding masses of grey cumulus: our *Lady of the West* pushed on, into the Thames estuary, over a glittering shield of finely-beaten silver four thousand feet below.

I wasn't sure what 'yes' or 'no' answer I could give. Annah is all feminine subtlety, you see, and her words are always either pleasant nothingness or contain the most grandiose of implications. So I looked up, and away. Anyway, it was cold, and southward on the Wash-like bank I could see where the citadel Hungry-gates squatted, monstrously, a fantastic conglomeration of monolithic keeps ringed by flying buttresses that rose up and fountained into cyclopean Doric architecture; its pentagon of faces gleamed with the polished pink of granite. Cunningly carved emplacements hid the batteries of gigantic steam cannon that guard the approach to our Imperial city.

New course set, I stepped up to her.

'Annah of Hesse, of Wales and the Deutschland's marches,' I began, retrieving the knife, chucked fingers under her chin, lifted it, 'you're a lovely lady . . .' I parted the curtain of her glossily dark hair and kissed her forehead and smiled blindly over the top of her head. I said: 'When my Weird is finally set upon me, and I am becoming inti-mately acquainted with the King's implements of torture, beneath the White Tower, then I shall name you "beloved", Annah Roman.' I tugged one of the coalblack loops of her waist-length hair, marched my fingers down the high, thrust-ing crest of her breasts, and smiled into her mercurial eyes.

44

My lady looked at me, green eyes oddly bright. 'We might tell a tale of glory to the King, Emmanuel. And sit among the Lords of Albion, once you'd reaped your share of what was harvested yesterday: for it was you who gave victory to the Empire.' An errant bumblebee buzzed impossibly across our wickerwork nacelle; perhaps it had mistaken Annah's ash-of-roses perfume for the fragrance of the living flower. Again, then, I remembered the scenes new-burned into my memory: our Navy appearing like so many phantoms outside Naples, and the antlike confusion of the Italians, since certain secret documents indicating that we were sailing to engage the Soviets above the arctic circle had, by a circuitous route, via myself, fallen into their hands . . .

For some time, even after our dirigibles phosgene-bombed their refugee ships, the cathedral, and the Red Cross hospital not far from Admiral Caraveggio's land headquarters, I had thought that their reluctant fleet dared not emerge. Though with a quarter of our admiralty's strength concealed below the horizon, or blinded perhaps by their foolish belief in the grace of God, the chances seemed to them the sort of odds professional gamblers *might* accept.

A fine plan. We feigned retreat; then our elite battle-cruisers, soft black feathers of smoke trailing behind them, lanced up from the south-west to make withdrawal impossible for their windjammers, and we burned their fleet and broke them . . . Annah was laughing, now, tinkling laughter as bright and hard as amber.

I shut the doors of memory, and locked away the memories of insect-struggles in the burning water below far below . . .

'Ay,' I said heavily, 'perhaps I will tell the king of glory. And perhaps then: "Arise, Sieur Emmanuel . . ." You would like that, wouldn't you?'

Amber broke, brittle. She turned away, walked off.

Sometimes I think that what I love is not *her*, but only my own Romanticized image of my lady of the West. And now, perhaps, I should tell you about her; the whole source of strength in me, the great love of my life, ever since I returned from several years' exile in Far Asia, much changed, writing *haiku* in flowing Japanese characters, into kung fu

45

fighting, bearing the long samurai sword that, to this day, never leaves me . . .

I knew her because I am a linguist, of sorts; specifically I could speak Welsh. And, returning to England to become a commissioned agent provocateur, I'd distinguished myself in the Troubles up in the North. Then résumés from the civil service's secret section had at last acknowledged me impeccable on the usual security counts, and their sovereign needed a man skilled in the black arts of espionage, violence, and the less theatrical sorts of blackmail and corruption, and so—

The King himself interviewed me: my fourth audience. The long arm of Albion had brutally eliminated the rebel Earl of Pembrokeshire, a Lord of the West, a month previously at one of the German courts. He was regretfully still extremely popular in the House of Sovereignty. Therefore the government's Act of Attainder against his sole heir, his Lady, had been ignominiously voted down. It had become a matter so delicate that the King wished me to root-out additional evidence against the Lady of Pembrokeshire herself, and to call on the royal cavalry, sack her mansion house, and bring her in chains to Londres.

That, Charles said, would present his enemies with a 'fait accompli', and should she meet with some accident on the long and arduous journey to us in the East . . .

I understood him perfectly.

Unfortunately, I fell in love with the lady, and only luck saved me from disgrace and probable execution. But Annah is so enchantingly beautiful she is impossible to resist: she wears her long hair like glory, sometimes black as ebony, or sometimes a fiery blend of metallic colours, as if coppers and rusts and golds were magically to become as soft and sweet-smelling as heather. Whenever she moves, she is as graceful as a swan. We're a striking, outré couple, I suppose, her blend of vivid colours and chunky rings and embroidery against my frosty-faced austerity, the loose black or white judo-robes I still wear, and that terrifyingly long sword dangling across my shoulders.

Even now, though, the King, or someone, forbids us to marry. We wait: sometimes I pray: sometimes Annah still hopes.

I soon found out she was nimble of wit; and she paints, in a luminous, chiaroscuro manner consciously evocative of Rembrandt; she loves music, deeply, as I do; she's quite a virtuoso on the harpsichord, and is almost magical with a flute. She is also very passionate, icily sardonic, full of doubts, wild, and her technique in bed is probably better than mine – perhaps the odd few years she's older than me account for it, but then I like to think of her in basically sensual terms, because she purrs and scratches just like a cat, is moody, never says good-bye, has claws . . .

She laughs much: a cool stream chuckling over stones; or when her nerves are stretched, like the sound of silver shillings flung as hard as you can upon a marble floor. Her palate favours foreign liqeurs, as mine does. I might add, she prefers sunrises to sunsets, which is the mirror of my own opinion; she also values Venus, the bringer of peace, above Mars, the bringer of war.

One of the unique things about her are her eyes, which are wet and sparkling and green-grey, and are windows which show you her soul.

She was and is wonderful. She is full of wonder, too, sweet as any child's. The exotic or brand-new, the odd sublimity in the beauties of Nature or in the human spirit, they never fail to exalt her.

I remember how she came to me, that first day two years ago when I hardly knew her: walking like a superbly-gowned spirit, whistling an archaic and haunting monody. I was sitting among fragrant lilac shrubs, beneath walls that were, then as now, carved with heraldic griffons and a lipping, worn frieze of Teutonic Eagle bas-reliefs. The wall itself is very, very old, and is cut out of the same dark and heavy-veined Cambrian stone that built all her Pembrokeshire estates.

Anyway, I looked up from my 'Northanger Abbey', to see faint clouds move as silent as ghostly galleons, in a sky of perfect blueness, and her. It was a magic moment: I was moved more deeply than I can say, though I think Annah sensed it.

We have never spoken of the matter.

Then, falling from a clump of low trees, moving to Annah's mouth-music, a host of what might have been bleached-white leaves swooped down in threes and fours, as she raised her unclothed arms to beckon. They were strange mutated butterflies. Soon hordes covered her with dew-dusted ivory tissue that was tremblingly alive . . .

A cuckoo called, somewhere. Then Annah, in her long gown of black and gold French lace, laughed and sang some more husky-voiced bars of music, and the flying creatures exploded from her like snow-flakes caught in a gale.

'So . . .!' I said, standing politely, then bowing, simultaneously tossing the calfskin-bound novel to one side.

We walked side by side through a copper-coloured coppice, avoiding the toadstools, then entered a sunshine-filled glade. I blinked as she spread rich scarlet cloths, and we sat down half shadily beneath a continuation of those same moss-encrusted walls. Before us a tiny Greek fountain chuckled a jet of water into a green, circular fishpond eye-lashed with white lilies, and half covered over with the pink and white and blue water-flowers of Far Asia.

'Music—' she said, and grinned cheekily as an urchin. She picked at a burr, or a knot, in her swirling hair. (Which was dyed deep russet then, I remember).

'A mouth-symphony, my dear?' I said, nearly sadly because my own defensive irony tasted bitter to me, and guilt was producing its time-honoured melancholia. 'You draw me,' I continued in the stilted manner of the Court, 'as the Sirens Odysseus, but I may not come: and my bonds, though abstract, are real. Duty.'

We silenced.

She began to unpack the picnic-basket she had of course brought.

I saw the water's greenness glimmer momentarily, heard a diving goldencarp *plop*: innocent, dartingly unaware, huge dragonflies flew by on irridescent gossamer wings. 'But then,' I said glibly, scratching the bridge of my nose, 'all is – "by the sweet power of music: therefore the poet Did feign that Orpheus drew trees, stones and floods—" and, see, Circe my enchantress, how you play the lyres of men's opened hearts . . .'

She coquetted to my courteous sally, but fear of my own honey lies had frozen me, and perspiration pricked unnervingly like needles of ice. Because I *dared* not play the

48

old games of love, not with *her*. So I sat back and let my hands hang loosely around my knees, and I thought not of her merry country tune but of the profound music of Bach and Beethoven, and I weighed that against hers and her lovely but technically less than adequate instrument, those cherry-coloured lips. I smiled to myself then, wearily, and shook my head, for there was poignancy that way. You see, there were giants in those days, heroes, and now, nothing.

'I am so lonely,' Annah whispered.

Nothing.

She tickled the bare skin above my ankle-bone, above the stylishly embossed leather of my boot, with a single yellow flower. I remember how uneasily I smiled, and looked away.

'At Court,' she sighed, 'all arts are beneath the finest, most generous lady Muses. Emannuel, do they still dance the pavannes and galliards of the first Queen Elizabeth? Are there still balls with a thousand glittering guests, and Lords and Ladies acting out their grand rôles in the theatre of reality, as we females display our finest wiles and plumage to all?'

I turned back smiling. 'There are, and they do. But, come now,' I said, as falsely sweet as saccarine, 'does Melpomene speak in you? Lady, surely you need have nothing to do with the Muse of Tragedy . . .'

I could have bitten my tongue out of my head.

I'd forgotten who the Lady was to whom I spoke, how she had suffered . . .

But she only smiled a wistful little moue, and murmured, 'Ah, how I would love to return there, to Londres.' She met my eyes, her mouth smiled archly, but behind her expression was a naked pleading, a burning anguish. I thought in desperation, Look, I *cannot* tell her that her life is a closed book, can I? Can I?

Nor that the Empire says to me: Kill this woman—

Two

It was cold. I let my two hands walk across the leather cases on either side of the piloting gear, thinking. Two massive cases: one held the intelligence reports, documents and souvenirs from Admiral Deschernes, diplomatic effects. I still had the choice, you see, and it would be so simple, to forego what we'd all sworn to do. So unnervingly simple.

'We grant to our servant Emmanuel Kyygard, for faithful service to the cause of Empire . . .' I hear him say it, as I eye the compass again. An estatehood from King Charles, almost certainly, for a victory of *this* gargantuan magnitude, for now we owned the Mediterranean. And the excuse would do: I would gracefully bow out of court intrigue and Imperial service itself, for I can no longer serve it with the quasireligious fanaticism my society demands. But in that future time, when I earn my bread by the sweat of others, there will be no more need of the King's pieces of silver, and I'll wash my hands clean of guilt, of hypocrisy, of the whole bloody business . . .

Looking down upon fallow fields, cruising slow, low enough now to pick out tattered scarecrows and individual clumps of yellow dandelions beside the hedgerows, I thought then of the summers of my lost childhood. Of lovely Cornwall. Of mornings when the sun would lie, golden, across wheatfields equally yellow; but when the western wind galed, I remember, I would think of the corn-ears as bearded, impudently tossing heads, and I'd clap my chubby hands together and laugh in delight. In September the sky is a scroll; its parchment was the leaden overcast that unrolls into the northeast from the Atlantic's wild white sea-horses of surf. Annah had ridden with me; at our tumbledown, deserted ancestral castle of Tintagel, I left a posy of fresh-cut roses on my parents' grave. Yes, there I would ask – would have asked – to be granted my 'place in the sun'.

I spat into the wind again, wearing an iron frown.

Temptation comes to us all, I *know*, but that vision was damnably seductive. Inwardly I fingered the magic touch-stone, duty, and I thought in sad anger, Ah, pale Charles, father of lies, lies—

South of the Thames still, we drew in sight of the outskirts of the capital itself, noticing the great grey sprawls of good English stone, the warm, ruddy brickwork, the spires and Imperial monuments. This: the greatest city of Europa and almost certainly of the world, even China or Brazil. Over half a million souls, they say. They say too that the Londres which was, long before the Fires, that our ancestors' city was still more vast, pointing out the hieroglyphic outlines still visible from high altitude. And perhaps 'they' are right, whoever they are; but I'll never know now, no matter how many self-contradictory encyclopedias I consult. I'll never know.

'Emmanuel . . .' Annah touched my arm, pointed, but despite my introspection I had seen. From our destination-of-record, the white Greenwich station, vast-hulled shapes were rising from their underground hangars, as threateningly grey as stormclouds. Yes, it's a magnificent spectacle, when a flight of skyships from the Grand fleet claws for altitude.

Absentmindedly I altered course to the northwestward, to overfly the Isle of Dogs and perhaps Limehouse, in quick avoidance. And crossed Old Father Thames. In the vee-formation of battle, the twenty-odd dragonshapes laid a course for interception: I glanced up from the compass, saw, was shocked numb.

'But – What is Kuard doing?' A cold hand, clenching inside my breast, froze off the words. Annah had gasped. I knew, then, what this might mean. And the falcons of the king raced for us, still rising as quickly as the pearl-like bubbles in weiss beer.

'Emmanuel,' she said, with overtones of fear casting a shadow on her words, and I didn't dare look at her face, 'it can only mean one thing. Those rumours drifting about in back-alley Ravenna . . . they have heard too; they think that someone, somewhere, against the Empire . . . has found an . . .' she choked, could not say the words.

'Impossible,' I snarled. 'No: this is a maneuver rooted in political crisis only. Eireland say, or some petty rebellion or assassin's plot . . . Unless they *do* know something . . .' my voice trailed off into silence. I knew that my face wore a glassy grin, but it had nothing to do with *me*, for fear churned in me, with another emotion more hateful still. I swayed to the heliograph, but another trellis-work of grey clouds suddenly covered the sun, drowning us in twilight.

Oh God, merciful one, cherisher of the meek, shield of the hapless . . .

She was almost shouting.

'Emmanuel ... we came back incognito ... They aren't expecting us for some days or more. The Fleet must imagine the *Lady of the West* captured ...'

God only knew what fears walked, what suspicions festered, now that the old Terror was loose once again.

The skycruisers mounted the sky ahead of us, outspread. Sun glinted from burnished parts as the lean sleek craft approached more slowly. Clearly they meant to drive us back, away from Londres. High over Ming Street I finally cut our power, a gesture of surrender.

'They might want us to put down at the Lea marshes ...' I thought with my mouth.

Or perhaps Greenwich itself, of course. My hands heaved on the steering bar; hydraulics groaned, and, rearward, the great black rudder, emblazoned with the heraldic ideogram of England's ruling house, the White Boar rampant, clicked in its lock-cogs and turned us.

Alicia of Aragona, the Duke's orphan who thought herself a woman already, tumbled out from the glass-panelled nacelle slung aft, her voice peppering us with a hail of questions that Annah tried to answer as soothingly as might be.

I thought of Cornwall, and the thankless future, as I slowed the engines' drumbeat, and when the sun disposed of its cape of grey I thumbed open the code-book to the cipher of the day and leaned across our heliograph.

THREE

'THEN,' I mumbled, fingers clasped on the flask of mulled wine, blinking bleared eyes, 'it is not merely gossip culled from some Gypsy riff-raff, but ... cold truth.'

We were all 'safe' at Greenwich now. Kuard van der Thorn sat in my cabin and shook a grey-maned, almost leonine head. Outside, through the bubble windows, I could see his own fleetship *This England* in another of the pens, aswarm with sweating, jovial mechanicals preparing her for flight. Then he stabbed at the map on the aluminium flaptable spread between us: at a collage of umbers and greens washed by sea-blues; foreign conurbations picked out in Cardinal red, trade routes cobwebbing in amber. Europe's patchwork quilt of statelets, cowed by the traditional red of Empire.

'No. Yesterday, the first accredited reports came in official sources. On the diplomatic front the Kaiser of the Deutschold affirms it, as do our consulates and the governors of our German provinces ... No.' He shook his head, and the lines on his face shifted as some profound, unfamiliar expression disturbed his legendary stolidity. 'The Austrian ambassador says nothing, knows nothing, but ... Vienna was – how can I say it? – destroyed. Blasted into nothingness. *Eighty thousand deaths* ...' his voice dwindled to a whisper, and I sat back uncomfortably, hearing in his tones rats' feet as they fared among dead grasses. 'My son Eli may have ... I ...' his voice cracked like a broken wineglass, fell in pieces. 'At Ferdinand's court, he was. And there is no word.'

'I am sorry,' I said, softly, after a moment had died, 'friend of my father, friend of me.' Then: 'Austria will be staggering in total confusion, all communications disarrayed. Do not give up hope. You must not give up hope.' My words, so grossly clumsy.

'Ay,' he did not even raise his frosty grey eyes from the map, 'you're right,' he lied. 'I have prayed, for the first time in my life, that it may be so, that Eli may be well. Many times. They seem only words ...' He looked away, emptily.

An awkward moment stretched until it broke. 'Is Hungrygates red alerted? And the Fleets?'

'What—? Yes, yes. But Emmanuel, a single night's work ...' He was holding my eye, and the faintest puzzlement passed over him as I must have – flinched perhaps – 'We must have dispersal, 'way across the Continent.' Authoritative again, he swept a heavy, age-scarred hand over the glossy paper. 'Londres is here, so central. Look, one single ... Bomb ... and our Empire would fail; collapse. The work of centuries, of how many lives.'

'Yes.' I coughed. The wine's fieriness licked the back of my throat. I stood suddenly, looked down again: at a pewter flask engraved in Cyrillic with the Boar carved obsequiously upon it. I looked again at the map, saw the shadow of a Boar rampant over all. That shadow was suddenly ringed with flame. For, one day, the shadow would be gone, and only the flame remain.

I thought of España; the Tagus glittering like snow-crystals in the early morning when Annah and I and a flamenco dancer and her guitarist, all of us from Seville, had begun a five hundred mile trek to Gibraltar; I thought of the coast of Barcelona where we'd transshipped for Portsmouth. And sipping my vintage, I thought of the other places, so many of them, so many. The Dordogne, Carnac and Navarre, spring along the Danube, and the Rhine valley where the golden flowers are the softest blanket imaginable under a drowsy May sun. Waterfront inns in the North, taverns like a dream of gold and smoke. Camus said that once, about Holland . . . I knew Europa, had roamed her, knew her secret places. I had found the true 'Europe', and loved her, for all that she was, for all the scabs men's sordid use of her had left, for all the surface cheapness and hardness-beneath it all, she was still beautiful, as she had been beautiful once, long ago when she was green and young.

Lying upon her now, gross and warlike and corrupt, Empire. Compounded of all the old evils of ambition and rabid nationalism – and how many crimes have been done in those names?

And yet . . . England, *my* England. What kind of a dilemma was this that came to gore me?

I unclenched my fists and looked at my family's old friend, who was gazing abstractedly down at the Imperial chart, not seeing it perhaps, thinking of his son who was lost. Somehow I was sure those stern old eyes could read me, see the twisted thing, the guilt inside.

I turned away, suddenly, walked to the ports and looked out at the energetic confusion of the Greenwich mooring station. I felt his gaze implacable on my back. 'I must see the King. What Machiavelli games does he plan, now?'

'Nothing,' his voice was flat, the words tumbled obscenely. 'No webs are woven. Emmanuel . . . if there is more to come, this may be the end. The end.'

I watched Annah in her long sable coat, three or four catwalks away, talking earnestly with some Negro. A triple gold ear-ring glittered in one ear; his Afric garb was strange, aggressively outlandish.

'Who is responsible? Does anyone know?'

Vice-admiral van der Thorn may have shrugged. 'Who

can say. But Ferdinand and his Archduchess had called a convocation of the powers of Europe. The armies-in-exile were represented there, of course. The Free Flanders regiments, the Scandanavians, the Germans, all those. And those who keep them in arms too, as sword and shield against the Imperial progress. France's Marshall of the Field, the nephew of the President of the Italian Confederacy, one of the Kaiser's highest generals, two Iberian counts. It may well have been a serious attempt to unite the Continent against us. Did you not know this?'

'My God. No, I did not!' Undermined psychologically, I turned away from the port and walked blindly back to my seat. Kuard's eyes were on me; but I could not meet them.

'Few do, of course. They wished to keep it deadly secret, but we heard, we heard. Admittedly, only those in the highest circles of government know it. But I would have imagined that *you* would've heard, Emmanuel. As a master of the sovereign's intelligence, and figuring somewhat high in the scheme of power-politics these days . . .'

I paused, shrugged. 'I've been away.' I frowned. 'But then – it seems our Albion is the prime suspect, eh?'

'*No*,' he said, erect in outrage, then shook his head, slowly, firmly. 'Never England. I cannot believe even Charles would – No. Not us. Someone else. I will not even consider "perhaps" . . .' He lapsed into brooding silence again. Not his only son. Not Eli. Not by the most malicious of all means. Not by an English hand.

To each his burden: to each his blindness. His patriotism was of the old order. And while he would always speak for England, right or wrong, there was a certain indefinable point after which he would feel he could no longer actively serve her. The murder of Vienna, alone, was far beyond this.

'I predict,' he said, 'enough pointing fingers, but a general rising of Europe is something else.'

I nodded. Kuard was probably right, their horror of the unleashed Fires or not. Almost certainly.

'But come . . .' he broke the mood, smiled with an aged charisma. 'I recall some mention of glad tidings of victory, hmmh?'

'Ay.' I cleared my throat. Already, the well-polished rhetoric of my story was beginning to bore me. 'The Italians planned with the Soviets in a bastard alliance against us; but I caught a—' I searched, '—hint of this, by the slow addition of whispers, and contrived to obtain a copy of their Admiralty's battle plan. Knowing dates and the rendezvous point, a part of our fleet lured them out from Naples before the Russian navy arrived: we had additional ships concealed beneath the horizon, who sailed nor'-eastward, entrapped those rather stupid tinsel captains without their Eastern ally, and sank the greater part. As for Naples,' I added as an after-thought, 'come dusk we bombarded the city until it was afire, as a prelude to withdrawal. From *The Lady of the West* it was like a hellfire sea. Lord Sidney thought that in light of their treacherous surprise-that-failed, a lesson was needed.'

'Their plan of battle, say you?' He looked at me sharply. 'But – how did you manage that?'

I shrugged three lives. 'A piece of luck. Now, Sidney takes the Fleet to scour the Eastern Mediterranean for the Crimean-based enemy's warships, though I fear he'll lose them. Deschernes and the flagship were lost.'

'Hmm. Not all good news then. I'm sorry to hear of it, he was a good man Deschernes. Sharp at the dice-table, a generous heart, polished manners. I knew him well when he was – commodore, it must have been . . .'

'Ay,' I said. Paused. 'I must see the King . . .'

He nodded. 'I have no time for more myself, Emmanuel. I am bound for the Continent—' there he stopped and reflected on something. 'But, certainly, you'll find the King at the Tower, not at the Chelsea Palace. With Whitesmith; they've summoned there the Council-of-Empire to discuss this – situation.'

'Thomas Whitesmith?' I had stood up but paused now, head cocked, smiling crookedly. 'Is not Manchester first minister still?'

'Emmanuel,' his eyes warned me, 'There have been changes, since you went away. Northumbria is now the second man of the Empire, and I'd be wary of treading too close to him.'

'Hmmh . . . What of Manchester, though?'

'They say Earl Hollingshead still occupies the White Tower—'

'A few levels below the ones he is used to?'

The tired old eyes flickered momentarily.

'There was some whisper of ... I don't know, intrigues, plots in cobwebbed family crypts. Or somesuch. Whether true or invented, Whitesmith is in the chair now, and Hollingshead is no longer.'

'Even the name,' I hazarded, 'Is no longer *à la mode*?'

'I take care not to enquire into such matters. As I said, Emmanuel, it is a time of changes.'

FOUR

WHEN we walked down the extending stairway outside the insulating cabin, the pens were all iron clamour inside vastness: a place of dragons. The next hangar's roof had been opened, and Kuard's own beast was now straining at the mooring lines, ready to depart. The flagship bellowed steam, and shrieked of its brute mechanical strength in spite of the flowing gracefulness of its lines. In one of the midships power-pods an Old salvaged diesel throbbed.

As we passed above, sweaty, grimed faces peered up at us from lathes and presses. Van der Thorn loitered, smiled down. I think his face was like a map of Passchendaele I saw once: contour lines of trenches that wrinkled on yellowed paper. The lines on his proud, eroded old face were faintly twisted with long-ago laughter.

'My Fleet,' he said to me, 'is configuring into a patrol-net. I myself will cast over to Brettaigné, help set up the best defense umbrella we can erect.' Nostrils flaring, he stared up at the leaden torpedo, incredibly huge and cloud-like over us. Two hundred, three hundred yards long, with the lifting capacity of giants, the grace of kestrels: the skyship *This England*, pride of our Fleet and scourge of the enemies of his majesty.

Again Annah caught my eye, fondling that Negro's leopard-skin doublet, laughing with him ...

'Frafric ... their Representative at Large, isn't he?'

'I beg your pardon?'

I motioned slightly.

'Ay. Look him up sometime, Emmanuel – the king will be

telling you more. He's got great plans, him.' Kuard nodded. 'To aid *this* one against the Soud Afrikaan fiefs. Then to glean easy pickings off the loser; finally strangle the victor with blockades; and raise the glory-flag of Empire.' He grinned, predatory again. 'Ay, it's "still waters run deep", with King Charles.'

'If you had plumbed those depths ...' I whispered, to myself.

'And Emmanuel,' he ploughed on relentlessly, deaf, perhaps half senile, 'I have been thinking. Charles is likely to be pleased with your work in Italia. The next time I see you, what chance you might be, say Marquis of Cornwall?'

I smiled, emptily.

'It might be. God go with you, Kuard. And ...'

He frowned, for several reasons.

'And?'

'Nothing. No matter . . . Good luck.'

'Fare thee well, Emmanuel ...' He climbed a stairway to the sky; willingly mustered hands dragged it away. A diesel roared throatily, and long plumes of steam trailed from the eggshell-smooth engine nacelle. From the workpits beneath, a few rusty cheers and whoops came up, ignorant patriotism speaking its imbecilic mind. The straining kite-lines were cast off from the skyship, and she rose as softly as a huge ball of thistledown, and soon glowed with afternoon sun-light. I climbed quickly up a gantry, onto the perspex roof. Effortlessly, she glided off to the south-east, still rising. I watched until his craft was a silver collar tailed temporarily there on the horizon; and then I turned away.

I knew I would never see him again.

Quickly I found Annah sitting tailor-fashion on a bench of plain, gnarled wood in a wagon yard behind; she was watch-ing the fire where some old silver-painted oilcloth from a skyship was being burnt in a heap. And as she watched, she swayed and sang an old song, a centuries-old, minor-key lament, in sad French. It was a long regret, over the dying of the religious Light: '... à Lyons, à Lyons ...' She sang of a Gothic cathedral, blasted, its great stones tumbling down; of the ritual burning of the Gospels.

My face twitched. I was about to throw some angry words at her, tell her to cease from singing *that* song, but I stopped. It didn't matter who might be listening. The danger was small and, more, it no longer mattered, really, if the King began to suspect I was one of the 'true believers' he detested so vigorously. I was through with Imperial service. One way or another.

So, instead, I walked across the grassgrown cobblestones and sat down beside her.

'Hello.'

'Hello,' she said, still staring into the quivering sun-yellow flames. And that was that, for a moment.

I said, unnecessarily, 'I go to see the king.'

She turned, looked at me solemnly. 'Do you think you will find out the truth?'

Later or sooner, it would make no difference in the end. I too peered at the warm blaze. 'I don't know. I *think* I have his confidence. It's hard to be sure, with Charles. I could tell you stories . . .'

'What, Emmanuel, what if the story is true, it was the Empire?'

I looked into the flames a moment without answering. Then I tried to find an answer that would not be clichéd, meaningless, flat, and dead.

'Then . . . we do what we must, of course.' I didn't really feel as if there was any 'of course' about it.

We watched the flames then. Bright and leaping, consuming everything.

She began to sing another song, even older, no one knew how many centuries old. A slow, sad ballad.

'*Hark, the drums do beat, dear love – no longer can we stay;*

The bugle-horns are sounding clear, and we must march away.

We're ordered down to Portsmouth, and it's many the weary mile,

To join the British Army – on the banks of the Nile . . .'

I thought of the eroded funeral mounds that men still call 'the Pyramids', for no real reason, and of the daughter of the Israeli army-general. Old memories . . .

'*Oh Willie, dearest Willie, oh don't leave me here to mourn:*

Don't make me rue and curse the day that ever I was born;

For the parting of our love would be like parting with my life,

So stay at home, my own true love, and I will be your wife . . .'

I thought of Annah.

'*Oh my Nancy, dearest Nancy, sure that will never do.*

The government has ordered, and we are bound to go . . .

The government has ordered, and the queen she gives command,

And I am bound on oath, my love, to serve in a foreign land . . .'

It too was about imperialism and war and sorrow. But it was all clear-cut, predictable, unavoidable – fate, destiny, Weird. A hard road one must travel down. The sort of philosophy my father would have accepted joyously, perhaps.

I shook my head. Things weren't that simple anymore. I knew you could read that in my face. Hard roads there were, but so many; one must *choose*, nowadays, choose some ideal that will define one's solitary path to commitment.

It was a long song, but it came to end eventually, as dark rainclouds gathered in the sky. The fire was dying too; large drops of moisture began to spatter down, and red embers hissed. So I stood up too, nodded, indicated that she should stay, and said, 'Yes. Yes, that was – quite beautiful, Annah . . . It helped,' I lied.

I squeezed her hand for a long moment, blew her a kiss; then, as she didn't say anything, I turned and left by the gates. She would back me, all the way, to the hilt. Whatever I chose.

Through the cherry-gardens, past a last sentry box, onto the cast-iron pier; there a long launch was waiting, which walked with six bladed legs upon the grey Thames. Backed by the tide, it took me to the shores of the city and to the antechambers of the king.

Inside the Tower a stentorian aide announced: 'Emmanuel Kyygard, colonel-in-chief of Intelligence, and high emissary of the king . . .' and I entered. Three men only were in the roomy conference hall: standing, Klaus Dekker, the German provinces' over-governor facing the uncouth and notoriously vigorous Duke of Northumbria, and, seated on a quilted-ermine throne, the king himself, Charles, effete son of the Empress Elizabeth.

'Ahh, our dear Emmanuel ... What news from Deschernes and the Fleet?'

I quickly knelt, kissed the offered ring. 'Your majesty, a great victory—'

Charles' eyes glinted as I spoke my picturesque quarter-hour long tale, but his mouth showed nothing at all.

'Good. Very good,' he said at last, judicially. He allowed some teeth to appear. 'You bring hoped-for tidings of good news, Emmanuel ... We will examine the reports you bring and would speak with you in private, later, on these things. But stay for the moment. We discuss the "German question", that old perennial. Also, there are some things which you must be acquainted with, shortly.'

I bowed, sketchily. 'I understand full well, sire ...'

Whitesmith rumbled heavily, 'Deschernes is dead, you say?'

'Ay, my lord Northumbria, lost when the *Prince of Wales* went down.'

'Hmm.' He turned his big blond head away, reflectively.

I could imagine his thinking. It's time for new blood; so that living museum-piece van der Thorn might as well be pensioned-off, because this is a *new* England now ...

I saw Klaus Dekker absentmindedly finger the multicoloured imitation windowpane. The stained glass in the Norman arches threw rainbows around the massive chamber, and its famous facetted-silver walls gleamed. Set upon the floor's rich Persian carpets was the mahogany conference table, polished to its familiar mirrorness where Northumbria perched, and several uncomfortable plaited-metal armchairs; very little else. A spartan ambience?

On the table I noticed the usual untouched ebony ashtray. The king gloweringly disapproved of tobacco. A portrait of the late Empress hung behind Charles' right shoulder; her mad jade-bright eyes followed you inescapably about the room. I stood at something like waried ease, and watched his majesty whispering asthmatically with the inscrutably-frowning Whitesmith, overriding his shaken head and mutters of 'no, by my oath'. Then the king hushed him with a gesture, and smiled demurely.

At some sleight-of-hand signal Dekker hinted at a bow, and began his setpiece speech. 'German nationalism is, in truth, reflowering, Majesty. Covertly: a little more stiffness in the dissension here and there, recently the development of a *"maquis"* of sorts in the backwoods ... The Deutschold and the still-free relics of the old Teutonic middle-Europe make no strong moves, secret or otherwise, but ... any major upheaval in the situation between Europe and the Empire and ... The Kaiser would *like* to seize the chance, of a united Deutschold once more, but whether he is strong enough, or the Empire ever weak enough even behind our unfortified frontier ... So: where are we going vis-à-vis our Reichland, to butcher a phrase?'

Affected, Frenchified speech – sickly-sweet, as far as our Duke was concerned. I could see that much.

'Mmm. I think ... Northumbria? ... a taste of our Dublin City regiments, hmm?' King Charles pursed his lips, steepled his fingers to Ely cathedral. 'Yes, a whiff of auto da fé, the death-kiss of mass reprisals ... perhaps some manufactured incident on our borders with one of the smaller fry of dukedoms, say a punitive raid ... thus let us plan, ay?'

Sieur Thomas Whitesmith, Duke of Northumbria and governor-general of the North, chief adviser to the king, shook his head annoyedly. 'Forget this about "our Irish wolf-hounds": of what relevance is it?' His tarnished fair hair still moved with the motion. 'What of Vienna? Vienna has been cremated by our Old-weapon bomb—' my world darkened for me, then, '—such a crime, sire, if it doved abroad, would inevitably raise all Europe. The fear of the catastrophic Old days returning is ... deep. *This* is the kernel, the king-issue. I did not travel through the night and the day from Newcassel to discuss putting some Hun chaff to the Question. We're not, after all, the Soviet Inquisition.'

I might have thought of the Earl of Manchester, below us in the Tower's black-rooms. It's unclear now; I have difficulty in remembering it at all.

'Yes,' said Charles IX of United England, of the Low Countries, High King of Eireland and Prince of Orange-Ulster, Vice-Emperor of Germany, Emperor-in-majesty of the Grand Empire, Duke of Brettaigné . . . 'Yes: we must find means of pinning the Austrian target, as a child would a butterfly . . .'

Cornwall: where all butterflies, they say, are born . . .

'Then . . .' he twisted one thin alabaster hand on the rich and fine-grained wood, 'we crush.'

'Ay, majesty, ay. But I propose we stay the while. Look, Europa is not united. Italia, France, Soviet Asia, *someone* will make the first move in carving headless Austria. Only then do we strike from our German provinces, using our massed Irish force, and seize the greater part. You see, the first one who moves – and I've no doubt that the Francais-bastard or someone is marching his armies already – we disclaim most vehemently, though not *too* stridently, note, in the pious name of all humanity. Others may well add their voice to ours, if we encourage the hope of making more pickings available on the Danube and Rhine axis.'

Coldly, now, came the regal 'Yes'.

'Europe is a pack of dogs. They fight one another while trying to bite the leash of iron we, one by one, lay upon them. For their pains they deserve a good whipping.' He smiled, his eyes flicking about to draw approval from our faces.

'Uhhmm . . . yes, yes, that is well planned, our good Northumbria. A Declaration might, if nothing else, cause the slightest fogging of the accusations, certainly if we seem slow to take advantage. Surprised, you might say.' He paused, became introspective for a moment. 'Very well; that is how we will play the game this time around. And how are the back-up arrangements for reinforcing our army in Antwerp progressing?'

Whitesmith sat back, smiled. 'Your majesty—'

FIVE

'—*À Lyons, à Lyons* . . .' echoed my footsteps as I walked the dank corridors of stone, there in the vast fortress centred around an ancient Keep. The new and the Old. I thought of psalm 137. In the stony quiet the echoes rang out the old, rang in the new, whatever it might be. From the fortress-city of Old York, soaring from the mossing-over ruins of our fortress of the Isle-de-France ... from Munick, Brest, Stockholm, Hamberg ... from all the strong-cities that were the ultimate guardians of the Empire ... the Council was coming. I rounded another crumbling corner, trod in twilight among stinking rush matting. From a chill alcove a cherubic linkboy rushed up bearing a tiny gas-lamp: and I nodded and began to whistle, softly '*À Lyons ...*'

Back at Greenwich I beckoned Alicia over from some flirting talk with a somewhat anaemic-looking Sky Fleet officer, and discovered Annah sitting tiredly under the craft's preburners. I kissed her, waited, then cast free from the pens. Some mechanicals waved as the bricked-over ground fell away below, two officers saluted with stiff formality. I waved back, leaning over, even smiled. And softly, as a thought in an empty room, we rose.

I turned the *Lady's* prow about, was facing westward, and dropped my hand to the power-levers. Slowly, reluctantly, we left the vast station behind, with its score or so of stranded whales, and crawled along the twisting silvery road of the Thames, heading into a blinding sunset. Into Rotherhithe I took the course of the old Jamaica Road, roughing-out in my mind's eye complex problems of 'windage', and the non-Euclidean geometry of roaring due east over the spherical world and still avoiding the gaze of Greenwich.

'Emmanuel,' Annah said then, after a moment, so that the wind-silence fell away, 'is it right, that we dare to do this thing?'

'Right', son of Man?

'Yes,' I said, slowly. 'The ever-changing wind turns about, to the north or south; but it moves in its circuits, as we do, under the instruction of God, moving to that Will. I *know* that now. I've got the strength to affirm, say "yes", even though the Light is dying. Our Lord the Risen Christ has few worshippers truly ... but ... I *believe*, that what we do now, the evil we resurrect, will also serve that immutable purpose. We must all do what we must. The kaleidoscope of God contained many pieces of vari-coloured glass. Each is a soul: each stained-glass tint is different. But together, they are the rainbow of His Will ...' Such pretty words.

But winds of hysteria were bursting from their brazen dungeons, armed with ice, in the brain's northern bleakness: I looked at their faces, and I only saw ghosts, or corpses animated with a pallid light, so temporarily that I could not call what we had 'life' at all.

Alicia snuggled between us on the command bridge.

'Annah, Emmanuel?' she asked. 'The Council-of-Empire is assembling in Londres: the king awaits. 'Neath the White Tower . . .' she shivered suddenly, like an October birch-leaf under the touch of winds, but laughed to hide it. 'The *White* Tower . . . oh God, when I think of the agonies, the vile things, the *obscenities* they do within . . . I . . . In the chocolate-coloured bolero jacket her ribcage was like flat wings of bone, opening, closing. Agleam with perspiration, her face was as pale as ash, her eyes too bright. I eased the rudder-bar and reflected that, for all she was our adopted daughter still, soon I'd be unable to shield her, though Annah might still comfort.

'Don't, Alicia,' Annah said torturedly. She held the girl close, kissed the top of her head, hugged her again. 'Don't, for you cannot relinquish your vow-burden. Alicia? Think of . . . hope. Of miracles. Because there *is* the Father, and a Kingdom of Heaven. Or think of what *we* did to Naples, Alicia. And hold on tight to the word "hope" . . .'

'Ay,' I said, roughly, 'don't cry, Lissy.' I watched a cloud-tower drift past, a dusty Impressionist mass, looked down at the miles-long waterfront of the capital. 'Please, please don't cry . . .' I knelt, then, and fingered the age-smoothed leather of the case, smelt its hide odour: and every stain or blistered discolouration, every cuneiform crack, seemed like a hieroglyph out of Time. My lean hands swept again across the heavy Portuguese leatherwork, knowing it was reinforced with steel mesh, and that the brass fittings disguised heavy antique electrolocks.

I straightened. Of the five other people who knew what the case contained or had found 'it', quite possibly two were already dead. Of all the conspiracies against the Empire, we, the smallest, were going to bring it down. Perhaps that meant something, somehow. I did not know. All my certainties had crumbled into dry dust. All my thinking had been done, the pitched battles fought on the grey plains of my brain: now both victors and vanquished had withdrawn from the field, leaving only stillness.

In a daze I pulled out my silver neckchain, and sorted through to find the correct key. An ice-bright memory leapt upon my back at that moment, rode me: of whispers, about the island cities of Japan, the flowery mountains I had myself found there, and then I recalled the poem had gone on:

> The wind circles us, turns our breath to stone;
> Each movement is an etch upon Time's mask.
> A bright moment traps us, change leads away,
> As if our moment had not scored the years.
> Yet: every shadow, each whisper, is not.
> For now, but for all Time, and Times beyond . . .

I had sat there for a long, long time, by the Adriatic shore, on the monastery's sands, while the winter wind rustled among the yellowing, spider-tracked pages, thinking. I do not remember that poet's name, any longer.

Then the key fitted, turned.

So I stood up and brought the *Lady* around in a slow circle over Westminster and Chelsea, and began to run away from the dusk. Kneeling then, I opened the case. Instruments glittered, inside: dials, bright metal and glass. Almost a work of fine art, full of the precision of Old workmanship; on a be-handled cask of silvery metal wrote a numerical inscription and some words of Cyrillic, the old language, not our modern pig-tongue.

'Emmanuel, God, tell me—' said Alicia, pain in her black eyes, 'I don't want to hurt you, or Annah. But I'm not a child. This . . .' she broke off quickly. 'Oh God, what are we *doing*!'

I touched the rim-rail, looked down on the green fields of the South. The Earth was my footstool, and from this height its faces were one. And consience returned, to haunt me with its ghostly pains. I helped our mass-murders in the Provence, directed the bombardment of Krakow; I played all the Borgia roles; I provoked the 'Milan Days' . . . Conscience: that's my Cross. How many nails called years, how many wounds called days?

I snarled suddenly. 'Alicia, be silent! I'm carrying enough

guilt on my back ... Do you think I could spy out the de-
fenses of Italia again, and block out the images that tell me I
am human? Or execute another held-hostage village in our
German holds, and by using excuse-words like "duty" and
"obeying orders" think it good?'

Silence wheeled down and exchanged glances, silence, like
the sound of a gull after it has cried. In an eye of the hur-
ricane calm, we passed over Blackfriars Bridge.

I wondered then if they would understand. Not Alicia,
Annah – but others, the 'they' who never die.

I straightened up, and said in a dully normal tone of voice,
'I must visit my parent's grave once more, after this is over ...'

These rituals are necessary, you see.

They looked at me, almost startled. I looked away, back
to the Thamesside landscape, slightly too quickly.

And Kuard, let us both hope you never search me out in
my hiding place, after this ...

Below, barges spread sails that were solitary red wings.
The low city slid beside us: moored ships, capstan-dotted
wharfs, cobblestoned spaces. Beyond was the metropolitan
forest of unwashed stone where crooked-looking spires
leaned upon the oddly low clouds. A great net of roads, criss-
crossing webs of lane and alley, with a few flower-gardens
and quiet, statue-haunted graveyards. And I saw people. I
saw faces, turning up, then down. Immemorial faces. I saw
England.

The Tower of London drifted into view dead ahead,
reflected brokenly in the water. When windows sparkled at
us I blinked.

'Alicia ...' winds rang out in that hollow pause. 'The
Empire creeps on, grows. But we are not gods, and so, like
that of Roma, or Bonaparte, one day our power *will*
crumble. All Europa will rise. And then the Tower will
reveal its ultimate secret. Not the racks, not the branding-
irons and thumbscrews ...' *The Lady of the West* swanned
down, over the ancient river, '—its arsenal of Old bombs;
nuclear bombs. This I say because I know the Empire, its
masters, I know how it will act.' I paused: 'And all the cities
of Europa – Oslo, Le Havre, Versailles – all those I know and
remember ... all will be consigned to the Fire, to save our

sovereignty. I cannot think how many people ... As Vienna ...' Words and worlds fell apart; set steady on the rudderbar, my hand whitened around the knuckles. I could only give a blind shake of my head. 'That must never happen, Alicia, no matter what the price.'

Oh God, it must not. Not a second time ...

I set the device, waited until Tower Bridge was coming directly below, then heaved it into the clean air and sunshine and balanced it on the gunwale. A push, and it fell away: Nine minutes forty-five seconds ... nine minutes and thirty seconds ... A plume of spray licked up an impudent tongue, close beneath the citadel's ringwall. And I eased us north-eastward, held the engines at their hysterical shrilling, went over Whitechapel, and due north. I looked down at the walking talking people who were already dead: a cloud of pigeons swept past us, and some grubby street-urchin raised a threatening fist. Then, past Mare Street, I raced us due east again, away from the grotesque light of the distended sun.

Annah Alicia Father oh Father ...

There were minutes and seconds and instants, and each were wounds.

After such knowledge, is there forgiveness? Forgiveness?

—Father, for I have sinned ...

He cometh up and is cut down, like a flower; he fleeth as it were a shadow, and never continueth in one stay. In the midst of life ...

We must all do what we must. The Cross. The nails called years.

I looked back at the orange dusk. Nothing.

In the west at last, a thousand suns – The whole cracked sky blinding white—

The world held its breath. Someone sobbed; a chaos of after-images was burning my eyes out; then the shockwave hit, tearing the tiller from my hands, blasting us into deafness. I collapsed, was flung onto Annah. For a long time we lay in the rush of scalding air and watched the horizon as it wrenched, sagged, jumped up, fell.

And I couldn't look back. At the lightness still unfolding from the heart of the darkness, at the boiling, twisting black clouds. I could only lie there, caught up in the killing web of history, and cry.

THE BONES OF BERTRAND RUSSELL

by

BRIAN W. ALDISS

'Anyone of a mind sufficiently enquiring to wish to determine the value of C Backwards must of necessity be courageous and dedicated – that a car mechanic should cherish this dream appears symptomatic of our civilization and of tomorrow's society. That he should also be bald adds a further illuminating comment. One should note that the Russell herein remarked in passing should not be confused with the third earl of that name.

THE BONES OF BERTRAND RUSSELL:

A TRYPTICH OF ABSURD
ENIGMATIC PLAYS

Futurity Takes A Hand

The scene is the upper left hand geranium garden in the grounds of the Escorial Palace, 39A Blenkinsop Road, Madrid, Brussels. FAN FAN CHANG *is talking to his android wife,* HI FAT GONZALES.

FAN FAN CHANG: I see in the papers that philosphers are back in favour. They are aparently very palatable and even people in modest income brackets are enjoying them.

HI FAT GONZALES: When you say modest income brackets, are you thinking of writing one of your enjoyable and memorable lyric poems round them, honourable husband?

FAN FAN CHANG: Certainly, unless anyone interrupts me.
On a modest income bracket
A lark sat down to sing
Every time you walk on a thistle
Heaven weeps at the injustice

HI FAT GONZALES: Lovely! I'll incribe it on my fan.

FAN FAN CHANG: It needs polishing.

HI FAT GONZALES: I polished it only yesterday.

FAN FAN CHANG: You're always complaining about how much work you have to do. I'm beginning to think you've ceased loving me.

A time machine materializes. A Time Traveller steps out.

TIME TRAVELLER: You won't believe this, but I am a time traveller from fifty years in your future.

FAN FAN CHANG: I believe you. How high does my reputation stand in your day?

TIME TRAVELLER (*aside*): Little does he know that I am his grandson. I am determined to shoot him.

HI FAT GONZALES (*overhearing*): But if you kill Fan Fan and you really are his gandson from the future, then you will cease to exist.

FAN FAN CHANG: 'Course you will, you fool. It's one of the best known paradoxes about time travel.

TIME TRAVELLER: My point precisely. My life is miserable, wretched. I am a complete failure. All my plans have gone wrong. I haven't a penny to my name, my hernia is playing me up, my friends have betrayed me, my wife has left me, I can't afford the new entropy kits. My hair's falling out too, incidentally, and I've got a shocking memory. My brother's trying to cross the galaxy backwards, if you please. Well, I mustn't bore you with my troubles—

FAN FAN CHANG *and* HI FAT GONZALES (*together*): But you have!

TIME TRAVELLER: Anyhow, my point is that I've come back here to kill you as the most painless method ever of committing suicide. When you die, I shall just – not have existed! Blissikins! I shoot you, and – bang! – or rather Pop!, I suppose one should say, to be onomatopoeically correct, I shall simply wink out of existence.

FAN FAN CHANG: Wait, wait, cue for a lyric!
The world's a funny place
For those with eyes to see
Only the other day I got
A wink out of existence

HI FAT GONZALES: It needs polishing.

TIME TRAVELLER (*draws gun from invalid chair secreted in his lap pocket*): Sorry to mess up your afternoon, but . . .

FAN FAN CHANG: Look out, there's an anteater behind you!

TIME TRAVELLER (*turning*): Where? Where? (FAN FAN CHANG *rushes at him and overpowers him, removing the gun*)

FAN FAN CHANG: Caught by one of the oldest tricks in the business. (*He points the gun at the Time Traveller*)

HI FAT GONZALES: Don't shoot, please, Fan Fan! I know he's our grandson, but I find I've suddenly fallen in love with him. It was that pitiful tale of woe, I suppose. Oh, grandsonny, I know I'm a mad impetuous fool, but I want to love you, to take care of you, I want you to sweep me up in your arms, to marry me – I want to have children by you, poets, little poets, lovely little wild poets and painters with cherry lips just like yours and legs like mine, endless children . . .

FAN FAN CHANG: Then I am deserted! Betrayed! I cannot face life without my darling Hi Fat. (*Shoots himself*)

TIME TRAVELLER: I can see this is going to be tricky . . .

CURTAIN

THROUGH A GALAXY BACKWARDS

The scene is a little chartreuse coathanger somewhere north of Tijuana Naval Base. Fred Astaire and Ginger Rogers are eating tacos. Two anteaters are dining on the remains of Bertrand Russell.

NELLIE (*reading the tablecloth*): It says here that fifty-one per cent of car mechanics are bald. Isn't that amazing?

ANGUS: It says *here* that the greatest Russian composer of the twentieth century—

NELLIE: It's no good talking to me about music. You know I hate it. Marquetry I like, but not music. It's always breaking into the bloody key of G.

ANGUS: *Not* always – is not Tchaikowsky but Irving Berlin. 899 songs, made millions.

NELLIE: I thought he was German. Did he ever break into the key of G?

ANGUS: My aunt Kit had an old telephone that used to break into the key of G in wet weather. Let's not argue, dear, it's such a lovely afternoon. Have this other leg, will you?

NELLIE: Isn't Russell delicious? Shows what philosphy can do for you. Frankly, I'm delighted we dug him up. Now philosophy I do like – almost as much as marquetry.
(*Enter MARQUETRY*)

MARQUETRY: You called?

NELLIE: How is it that whenever you come on stage I start thinking of that Chinese lyric by Fan Fan Chang?

MARQUETRY: Does it have anything to do with the fact that I'm wearing this stupid cheongsam? Is it because Angus is eating fried rice with his Russell chop suey? Could it be because Betty is playing chopsticks? Does the fact that you have The Collected Lyrics of Fan Fan Chang open before you have anything to do with it? I ask these questions with a tolerably open mind, being always reluctant to come to definitive conclusions about anything. Without wishing to strike too sapient a posture – which would probably ruin this bleeding cheongsam – I would define my position as pragmatic unpositivist, with the accent on the 'ist'; if more people were of a like opinion, then the world would be a happier place. (*Exits*)

ANGUS: You were going to recite a lyric poem, my dear.

NELLIE: How is it that whenever that stupid little pragmatic unpositivist leaves the stage I forget a Chinese lyric by Fan Fan Chang?

ANGUS: How many lyrics by Fan Fan Chang do you know?

NELLIE: I forget. On the other hand, I do remember reading the other day that a man in a spaceship had gone through the galaxy backwards.

ANGUS: How very unpleasant for him. How did they know?

NELLIE: They watched him through telescopes, I presume. He was only an ordinary car mechanic, too.

ANGUS: Ah, then he was probably bald.

CURTAIN

WHERE WALLS ARE HUNG WITH
MULTI-MEDIA PORTRAITS

The scene is a palatially furnished bathroom in the gardening pages of a certain notorious newspaper (not the one you are thinking of, but a similar one which recently went up in price). Hitherto unknown varieties of plant decorate the room. The walls are hung with multi-media protraits of bald car mechanics. A crowd is gathered.

CROWD: Moo!

(*Enter* STEPHANIE YEOBOUGHT)

STEPHANIE: Ladies and Gentlemen, it is given to few in their time to have the privilege of standing before you as I do today, nobly and impartially, and in all due modesty, yet with a proper sense of occasion – it is given to few, I say, to be able to announce before thousands and many of them themselves distinguished in their own way, too – women of charm, men of accomplishment, children of distinction, yes, yes, even lapdogs of outstanding merit and not unknown at Cruft's (*laughter*) – to be able to announce, I say, that on this very day, this happy day, the event for which we have all been waiting – waiting for moreover, with an almost unbearable sense of impending fate and futurity within the cherished privacy of our own homes – nothing less than the rediscovery, at the bottom of a humble anteater's hole in Piccadilly, just where the south end of Glasshouse Street comes out under the big Coca Cola sign, now scheduled for preservation as part of our great national heritage – the rediscovery, I say, of the sacred bones of Bertrand Russell, last of the playboy philosophers. (*Wild cheering, lascivious laughter, the skirl of the pipes, ties thrown in air, stamping, the ejection of a male for reprehensibly taking advantage of the uproar in that he did goose a lady standing in front of him. The lady follows.*) Oh, and I forgot to mention it, but Ronnie Hicks has just been round the galaxy backwards. (*Cheers and mutters of 'Piss off Ronnie Hicks'*).

(*Enter* RONNIE HICKS, BACKWARDS. *Clutches his joysticks*)

RONNIE HICKS: It was nothing really.

VOICE FROM BACK OF CROWD: Speak up!

RONNIE HICKS: Sorry, it was nothing really.

VOICE FROM BACK OF CROWD: Then why did you say it, you scientific bastard?

REPORTER: Mr. Hicks, in the light of your great achievement, may I just ask you about your family genealogy. It's a little complicated isn't it?

RONNIE HICKS: (*defensively*) Not necessarily. People go on about my brother being his own grandfather but I don't see anything funny in it.

REPORTER: I was thinking in particular of a lyric by the poet Fan Fan Chang, who died this century—

VOICE FROM BACK OF CROWD: Last century, you nit!

REPORTER: I meant last century. But after all, if Fan Fan Chang had shot himself only twelve hours later, it *would* have been this century, since he did it on the afternoon of December 31st in the last year of—

SEVERAL VOICES FROM BACK OF CROWD: Get on with the bleeding interview!

STEPHANIE: The lyric of which he is thinking, Mr. Hicks, if I may interpolate a word at this juncture, is the one that goes

As I was going to Andromeda

I met a man with seven children

Everyone of them was each other's grandmother

And my brother is also my uncle's stepson.

I mean, legend has it that the reference is, in a word, to you yourself. Can you confirm or deny that?

RONNIE HICKS: You're a lot of muck-rakers, the lot of you. I came here to speak about my recent amazing scientific achievement, and instead you want to pry into my private family life. Typical, bloody typical. Nothing's sacred. Where's the light of scientific wonder shining in your eyes, burning there like a precious flame or sapphire? My brother, if it interests you, married a wonderful woman, my sister-in-law and grandmother, who bore him dozens of little poets, lovely little wild poets and car mechanics, with lips like cherries and a tendency to baldness – one of whom was me. I'm proud of my background. Without it, I doubt whether I'd ever have been able to travel round the galaxy backwards.

REPORTER: I meant to ask you, what was it like?

RONNIE HICKS: You've offended me. I'm not going to tell you. (*They fight. The* REPORTER *jumps on* HICKS *and pummels him till he gives in*) Okay, okay, I'll tell. Just let me get up. (*Rises*) Well, first let me say that it is given to few in their time to have the privilege of standing before you as I do today, nobly and impartially—

VOICE FROM BACK OF CROWD: Cut it short!

RONNIE HICKS: It was terrifying. I seemed to see all the events of my life crowd before my eyes in quick succession. Outside, there was almost total darkness. My craft was bucketting wildly. The instruments were not responding. You must realize that at this time only the speed of light forwards was known; nobody knew the speed of light backwards. I saw the great galaxy itself, yea, all which it doth inherit, fading into something no bigger than a pinball machine and vanishing into a corner that looked for all the world like your back passage. It was pretty scary. My two fellow cosmonauts – also car mechanics and bald like me – were either dead or dead drunk. It was a moment for quick action. I climbed into my suit and made my way outside on to the hull, intending to release the oxygen tanks, when I realized I had already done so. Time was going backwards as well as space. All I could do was hang on, not lose my nerve, and wait.

REPORTER: And when did you actually get back?

RONNIE HICKS: I think it's tomorrow. Not an experience I'd care to repeat, let me tell you. But, after all, research must go on, there must always be a few intrepid men willing to risk anything for their fellows. (*The crowd begins to drift silently away*) The spin-off in terms of technological advancement from all this will be immeasurable, not least in the region of anteater-breeding. (*Now everyone has gone except* RONNIE HICKS *and* STEPHANIE YEOBOUGHT) New perspectives have opened up to us. We pause in awe on the threshold of a new age.

STEPHANIE: I'm afraid I also have to go now. I have a speaking engagement. (*She begins to put out the lights*).

RONNIE HICKS: It's been wonderful ... (*He tries to look into her eyes*)

STEPHANIE (*breathlessly*): For me too. I hardly know what to say.

RONNIE HICKS: Life's too short, my darling. Did that thought ever occur to you?

STEPHANIE: No. How do you mean, too short? Do you mean you're longer than it is?

RONNIE HICKS: No, I just mean that – well, that life's too short ...

STEPHANIE: Were you born at the age of ten or something?

RONNIE HICKS: No, no, not that exactly. I just mean – well, we don't get enough years. Let me put it that way. We don't get enough years.

STEPHANIE: Sorry, perhaps I'm being dim. You mean if you counted them some would be missing? By the way, how long were you away, travelling round the galaxy backwards?

RONNIE HICKS: Let's go and have a bite to eat and I'll tell you all about it.

STEPHANIE: I know an adorable little place at the south end of Glasshouse Street, darling.

RONNIE HICKS (*shyly*): Darling! (*They embrace. Enter large Space Vehicle, backwards.* RONNIE HICKS *emerges*)

CURTAIN

ON THE INSIDE

by

ROBERT P. HOLDSTOCK

Robert Holdstock last appeared in New Writings in SF volume 20 with MICROCOSM, and is represented here by a story which evidences his interest in the incomprehensibility and duality of life. If you are not the man you think you are, must you necessarily be any other? Must periods of blankness necessarily have a greater meaning than blank pits of fear? Andrew Quinn, who kept his wife in the closet, had no reason to doubt the yin and yang of his rediscovered life – until – and then – but real life cannot be wrapped up in neat square-sided packages tied with pink ribbon, as the eminently satisfying snapper to this story shows.

ON THE INSIDE

ONE

A DAY like any other day.

Andrew Quinn sprang from his foam rubber cradle and crossed the room to the shutters. The shutters opened before he could touch them and daylight illuminated the untidyness of the small apartment, made him blink as he reached to drop the polarizing filters.

It was going to be a good day, he had that feeling.

Naked and wide awake he crossed to the wall closet, opened the door. Unzipped one of the plastic coffins that lay within and kissed his wife good morning through her polythene shroud.

He felt a momentary sadness – their life together had been so short and they had accomplished so little – and then he zipped her up and closed the closet. He should have said a prayer or two, but it was too nice outside and if he hurried he would get some sun before he had to plunge into the cool of his office.

He dressed and shaved, performing both operations with speed since both necessitated a certain amount of mirror work and his gaunt features and wasting frame were something he would rather not face when he was feeling in a good mood.

Easing himself into the kitchenette he ran his usual spaceship fantasy, and began to operate heater and cooler controls as if they were drive controls. Sinful thinking, he knew, but there was only a one in a thousand chance that he was being listened to at that precise moment.

He prepared coffee, sweetened with fermented honey and a twist of butter; he consumed three rounds of toast, made a drink of vitamin and trace mineral supplements, and then closed down the kitchen unit.

Easing himself out of the kitchenette he read his mail, which today was three happy-leaflets (which of course he *didn't* read) and a modest advert for underwear. He was expecting news from his brother in Manchester but since mail from the north could languish in the censors office for anything up to a month, he was hardly surprised when the letter failed to materialize.

He might try and use the work holophone today, his own being a local phone only, but there was a stiff penalty if he was found out and he was already in trouble with the authorities for using insulting language concerning the Church.

He was always in trouble for insulting the Church, but it was usually the monitors which reprimanded him; this time a faith-patrol policing the area near his apartment had heard him and decided to get nasty. One never argued with a Churchwoman. They were less tolerant than the police. Quinn had argued vehemently and been booked, but he had later confessed and now would not appear before the criminal courts for several months.

And in the meantime he was unbothered about the situation. The wavelengths made sure of that.

Checking his time on radio City he left his apartment at precisely nine thirty and caught the in-town magnit at nine forty. It was packed with commuters, of course, and a raucous good humour pervaded the compartment. Quinn joined in the early morning banter, hanging on for dear life as the train twisted its way along its razor thin rail.

By the time he arrived at work he was in such a good frame of mind that his office, a small dark room at the back of the building, was a welcome sight. He worked hard all morning, eliminating his in-tray in two hours. By twelve fifteen he was on his way to Hammersmith open-park and he joined the queue for his allotted spell in the giant preserve at twelve thirty. It took just a few minutes to gain access to the park which meant he had a little over twenty minutes to roam before he had to leave. Because of what had happened the previous week he faced the gates with just a tinge of apprehension, but he flashed his identity card at the monitor and walked rapidly past it and

Shock.

His knees went out from under him and he struggled to keep his balance. Someone grabbed his arm and murmured, 'All right? Need any help?'

'No ... no, thank you,' he shook his head and tried to merge with the crowd, to escape the eyes of the man who had seen him stumble. He stared across the grass, at the milling crowds, at the rustling trees. His head was filled with noise, with confusion, with fear. He had one thought – the diary!

After a moment he grew calmer, and his thoughts became clear. The diary. He had to get to the diary.

He began to walk swiftly along the lakeside. Without really knowing where he was going, remembering places as he reached them, he came inland to where tree covered slopes gave a measure of shade to the grass, and to the hundreds of people who lay sprawled upon it, overlooking the narrow, winding stretch of water below.

He hesitated, getting his bearings. He listened to the buzz of conversation, to the sounds of trees and laughter. There was a strange murmuring above all these sounds and something in his head said: Monitors.

He didn't know what Monitors were, but he felt afraid of them.

He paced up the gentle slope and into the trees and after a moment he noticed *his* tree, his special tree, a large preserved oak, very very old and quite obviously dead. There was only one man sprawled beneath it and he was half asleep.

In a hole in the base of the trunk was his diary, pushed as far in and up inside the trunk as his reach would allow, to where there was a small ledge. Making sure that no one was looking, he reached in, felt around and located the small book. With growing excitement and a noticeable activity of his heart he pulled it out and stared at it for a long moment.

Hiding the diary with his hunched body, he pretended to be dozing as he read the contents.

The first entry was a hastily scrawled opening testament:

I can't remember my name or who I am, or where I am, or what I am, I'm just here suddenly in a park, and I know I'll have to leave the park though I can't figure out my motivations or why I'm so afraid of the television monitors that are scattered about. This diary belongs to Andrew Quinn which is me, but I have no memory of anything earlier than a few minutes ago. I'm just here, suddenly and with incredible feelings of familiarity with the whole place, but with nothing in my head except vague fears, vague uneasiness and a language. Feelings: frightened and alone.

The final words were scrawled so badly that he had difficulty making them out. He felt less frightened today but still very lonely and with incredible feelings of loss.

He thought very carefully and then wrote:

When I left the park I lost myself in blackness and I was not fully aware again until a few minutes ago. I became vaguely aware of fear several times, and I remember these times clearly. I seemed to be dreaming and there was a small room filled with furniture and very untidy, and the dream was happening all around the room. Otherwise I seemed to be looking out through a haze – nothing was real, nothing had solidity. I am accumulating information slowly but I still have no notion of what or who I am, or even if I belong; there is a starkness about this park and I notice uniformed and armed attendants, a lot of them women. I wonder if in someway I am suffering from an illusion in my every day life that dissolves suddenly when I come into this park. It's my only explanation. Everyone is happy but I'm terrified and probably very conspicuous. I am obviously the only person who is seeing this sort of reality. I am afraid to leave the park because it means I will be made unconscious; the time lapse seems very small but the shock of becoming so suddenly aware is very great.

That was as much as he wrote before he noticed everyone around him was moving off towards the park exit. He hid the diary back inside the tree and walked along with the crowds. Again he felt uneasiness as swivelling monitors perpetually turned to look at him. Again he felt familiarity and yet nothing concrete came to mind.

As he passed out of the park he fell back into darkness.

Quinn returned to his work and later in the evening to his small home at the edge of the city. He spent the evening watching television, a five hour play about life in a monastery in Devon. The sermon was a familiar one, although the story became a little risqué at times and was worth watching.

He became very relaxed. His neighbour, Steven Fabin, called in for a game of chess and ended up watching the last hour of the play before departing with Quinn's promise of a game the following evening. Quinn turned down the lights in the room and brought his wife out of the closet and laid her before the Resurrection Icon, a large portrait of Michael preparing for the final battle with the forces of evil who could be seen amassing themselves in the dark heavens above earth.

Quinn prayed long and hard, and his prayer left the subject of his wife and turned to him, and it was five minutes before his conscience pricked him and he stopped his indulgence.

He put his wife away, struggling slightly as he manoeuvred her body into the narrow closet space, and then he went to bed. He lay in the darkness thinking of his second blackout; he was only vaguely aware of the soothing voice in his ear whispering reassurances.

In two or three days the fact of his second blackout was of historical interest only. As his park allotment came near he felt apprehension, but spent some time in a mirror booth and emerged cleansed and high spirited. He had not confessed his trauma.

Shock.

He was back in the park. People milled around him and he felt unsteady, but the disorientation was only momentary. He moved along with the crowds towards the lake and the tree covered slopes. He looked at the faces around him. They were all smiling, all happy. He must have stood out a mile.

He listened for birds, as he walked, and was aware that there were no birds. The trees were real enough, as was the grass. There were insects in the grass he noticed. The park was quite authentic.

Someone was half asleep beneath his tree and he moved over as quietly as possible and reached in through the hollow. The diary was there and he removed it, rolling onto his stomach and turning away from civilian eyes; as far as he could determine no monitor eye actually watched this spot.

Opening the diary he felt his heart miss a beat as he read his previous entry, and then he wrote:

It goes on. There are seven days between park visits. I'm terrified, but only because this is so unnatural. I can't understand whether I'm all the same person leading two awarenesses – literally – or whether I'm two people. I have no feelings for a man called Andrew Quinn. But I *have no* other identity.

He got no further. The man beside him woke up and sat up, staring at him. He was forced to hide the diary and act disdainfully until the other man moved off. By the time he was on his own again his time in the park was finished.

For the rest of the day Quinn felt very disturbed. The blackout whenever he entered the park had now happened three times. What was worrying was that he did not just keel over and wake up in a hospital – no, he woke up actually walking through the gates! So what on earth did he do during those few minutes he was inside the preserve?

His colleagues seemed oblivious to his distraction and by mid evening, of course, he was soothed and immersed in a game of chess with Fabin. Quinn lost, but more through Fabin's skill than his own worries affecting his game.

When he faced the park a week later he was almost terrified, but he was determined to conquer his forgetfulness, and he stormed through the gates . . .

The transition was getting easier. He made straight for the tree, slipping and sliding on the grass which had been soaked by the morning's rain. He reached in for the diary and opened it, making ready to write . . .

Shock.

There was an entry *after* his last entry. He read:

I don't know who you are and like you I don't know who I am, or where I am, or what I am, but I'm terrified. I came to this tree a few minutes ago because it seemed familiar. I found your diary and suddenly I feel, well, full of hope. Excuse my scrawling, but I've got to get it down before I go under again.

The same thing is happening to me as is happening to you, I think. I come into this park and I sort of wake up. There is a frightening familiarity about this whole place, this tree especially. But my memory is non-existent. When I'm not awake I'm in limbo, aware yet not aware. I see vaguely through my body's eyes, I see myself doing things, talking to people, working with people, walking and relaxing, but it's all blurred and it all seems totally aimless. Listen, I don't have a name. Right now I can't remember a thing about myself. I just exist in this body and whatever control is exerted over me outside the park vanishes only this one time every week. It's all I have. What do we do? How can we meet?

Two

IT WAS almost too much for him. His head began to spin, and he felt the signs of a faint coming over him. But he kept conscious and his head cleared. Someone else like him! It was almost . . . almost too good to be true. A shot in the arm that he needed like no shot he had ever received before. A shot in the arm . . . needles, injections . . . where did he remember such things from?

After a moment he wrote:

My name is Andrew Quinn and I live at 39 Houndel Street, East Sector Five. I remember a few things about my existence outside the park, but only a few. Like you everything is very blurred and though I'm obviously in control right now I just can't remember much about my outside-park life; when I'm outside the park I obviously remember nothing about now because it's a tremendous shock coming into the area. When I just read of your feelings of familiarity , it hit me too. This tree meant something very long ago. I can't remember what. And the lake – does the lake seem familiar to you? I seem to remember a group of men in grey coveralls down by that lake. Does that mean anything?

He saw his park time was finished and hastily secreted the diary. He wished he could write faster. And the pencil was getting blunt and how was he going to think to get a pencil sharpener?

As he approached the gate he became aware that somebody was watching him. A man of middle height and middle years, slightly fat and very solemn. When he caught Quinn's eye he turned away and lost himself in the crowd.

There was very little time left before he passed through the gates. He searched his pockets again but found no writing implement. He had not dared to take the pencil from the diary in case he returned without it next week. And he *did* need a sharpener . . .

On impulse he spoke to the man walking next to him. 'May I borrow a pen for a moment?'

'Sure.' He passed Quinn a small, silver pen that had the finest point he had ever seen . . . and where had he seen others, he wondered as he wrote 'pencil sharpener' on his wrist?

He passed the pen back and smiled. 'Memory jog,' he said, and the other man smiled back.

Later, sitting at his desk, Quinn stared at his wrist and felt very ill.

'What's the matter, Andy?'

Quinn looked up at his office colleague. 'I don't know. I've got the words "pencil sharpener" written on my wrist. I'm damned if I can remember writing it.'

'Pencils!' his colleague laughed. Quinn's collection of ancient pencils was better known than Quinn himself. He had, for a time, boasted their uses, and even written letters about them to the fax's. He had hoped to get pencils re-introduced, but in fact there was no advantage to such an implement. Everwrite points had been around long enough for them to be taken completely for granted. 'You haven't been looking too well, these last couple of weeks, Andy. You ought to apply for more park time.'

Quinn felt cold. 'That's something else again.'

'What's that?'

Deciding that it might not be good policy to mention that he couldn't remember having been in the park the last three weeks, Quinn shook his head. 'Nothing.'

By the end of the afternoon he was bright and cheerful again, and the nagging feeling that he was ill had passed. He squeezed onto the 6.10 Eastbound magnit, joined in the chatter as they sped out of the city, and by the time he arrived home he was feeling like some action.

He knocked up his neighbour, Fabin, and they trotted down to the fun palace, which was conveniently only a twenty minute walk away. Fabin did not have a nightwalk permit for that evening, but they'd taken such chances before.

Indulging themselves at reasonable price in the pleasures of flesh and mind, they staggered back together singing the praises of the Church, and making up dirty rhymes about the monitors. It was all perfectly normal and they did not fall foul of the law.

Home again, Quinn stared for a while at his relatives, stacked neatly in their coffin slots, and then, his due respects paid for the night, he went to bed.

By the following week he had forgotten his apprehensions and faced the park with a renewed determination to beat the blackout.

Disorientation ...

The diary! Quickly, quickly ... Quinn began to walk as fast as he could without having any obvious direction.

The tree was there, and he had to wait a couple of minutes to squeeze into its shade. When no-one was looking he reached in for the diary. Nearby someone was reading a single-sheet news bulletin.

He read the other person's entry quickly and excitedly.

Yes, even as I read what you had written I could remember. Six or eight men in grey overalls, doing physical exercises or something strenuous. I have a recollection of exercising too.

My name, I've found out, is Dan Farmer. I work in an office in a government centre dealing with publications. I tot up figures most of the time. I managed to find these facts out, but it's all I found. I can remember this tree, though. I used to spend a lot of time under this tree with two friends. I can't remember them very well, I just have vague recollections of conversations and excitement. One of them was called ... Pierce? Something like that. We used to talk about stars. Does that ring a bell? It's all I have. Just stars, sleepy conversation – and the three of us. Think about it.

Stars!

Pearson, Fletcher, Stormaway ... and Burton!

Space flight. The *Oriel*!

It was all there ... no, not all, just the beginning. The beginning of a memory. Burton rolled over on his back, tears welling in his eyes.

The flight, remember the flight, the excitement. What a journey! Deeper into space than even unmanned satellites. They'd gone to Proxima C. but that was as far as they'd gone. Then they turned back ... and what happened? What happened then?

Burton wrote:

My name is Ray Burton and I was proximity-navigator on the *Oriel*. I don't know if you are Fletcher or Stormaway, but the three of us used this tree as our office. We had plans ... we had such plans – remember? We were going to spacewalk round Proxima C., but by the time we got there there were too many other things to do.'

He drifted into memory, a curiously shortened memory. There was a bulky shape spiralling against the star strewn night, faces watching the figure from a dim-lit cabin.

There was no more. The memory was fragmentary. He had been thinking so much that he had lost his allotted time. He hid the diary and began to walk swiftly towards the gate.

On his next visit he could hardly keep his body in control. He wanted to run, to leap, to shout as he tore across the grass to the tree. But he kept calm. The diary was still there and the other man's entry was scrawled and hasty, but Burton read it with stomach knotting.

Is it really you Burton? My God. What happened to us? This is Stormaway. What happened to us? Where's Fletcher, the others? Christ, Burton, what have we got ourselves into?

My host is a real drag. Just recently I've been able to spy through him a bit more. He never drinks, never goes out, never has women in. I'm trying to prod his lust centres a bit, but I can't find the location. If he'd only take an occasional sip of rum . . . I've got a double park allotment today. I was looking pale, and I'm not surprised. With my sort of narcissism anyone would look pale. I'm also leaving this pen . . . the pencil has just about had it.

Hey, I'm rambling. I'd better calm down. Plenty of time today. Is this *really* the London we left? So many people. I never knew there were so many people! Right back to the bad old seventies. And so happy. Did you ever see such programmed happiness? My hero, big do-no-evil Farmer, is forever singing the praises of the bloody government and the bloody Church. Lot of women in power, but I don't think we're in a Matriarchy. There are little sub-conscious jingles playing all the time. These people are brainwashed, every minute of the day. Except in the park. Perhaps the mind needs a break. As you can see, my awareness is growing, but I never remember the park until I get back here. I have a card that tells me about my double allotment. It isn't dated. I wonder if I can keep it for another day?

Is it possible we can get out of the depths of our hosts' minds because this subliminal barrage ceases? Or is it the familiarity? This park is the only thing I recognize in the whole goddam city. It was very new when I knew it before. We did a lot of training here, didn't we, while we were on theoretical courses in-city?

I remember bits of the flight. And the fight too. Jesus,

we said some harsh words, Burton, and I wish we could say a few now, just for old time's sake.

I get the impression that space flight no longer exists, a sort of sin. The society is intensely Christian – in fact it's almost Chardinian. They all believe in this Omega Point nonsense; Christianity expressed mathematically, I suppose. They don't contraceive, they don't abort, they don't euthanise, they don't leave the planet in case they're not here for resurrecion. It's incredible. We *were* only away three hundred years weren't we? This tree is dead, the wood hardened artificially, I've figured that out. Good job, eh? Without this tree ... what? What can we say? That we wouldn't be enjoying ourselves so much?

My time is nearly up. Listen, Burton, we've got to get the hell out of this place. How do we do it? Obviously we've got to get control of our hosts, but how? Patience? I'm losing mine. I feel the symptoms of claustrophobia developing already.

That was all.

Burton looked about him. For the first time he noticed the large number of religious icons that adorned the colourfully dressed populace. It had never really penetrated to Burton's awareness that his host – Andrew Quinn – was a low status individual living in a Church-dominated society. And what Stormaway had said about the sinless existence, or rather, the lacking of sensible precautions against overcrowding. Did that mean that Quinn's trips to the fun palace (which Burton had detected vaguely, had believed had been real, and had enjoyed) were they in fact just illusion? Was the illusion of sex less sinful than the actuality? And the zipped up wife, the horrible yellowed mummy lying in its cellophane coffin, and the other bodies, neatly stacked within Quinn's living space ... bodies preserved for resurrection? Cheap burial?

Burton wrote:

No time for length. I'm going to try and gain time by hiding in the park. I'll look for you next time you're here. If you don't hear again, something went wrong. See you in hell ... I have also wondered about the others. Thank

God, though, for the small mercy of having made each other's contact.

He hid the diary again and walked deeper into the wooded slopes. People milled around and he felt slightly conspicuous because they were walking towards the gate and he was not. He kept his attention centred on passing park attendants, moved out of their way as much as he could. Monitors turned slowly and he felt sure his progress must have been spotted, but no alarm was raised, no-one came running for him.

Deep in the trees, with the next shift of visitors streaming upwards towards him, he sat down and shivered.

Hours went by, crowds came and went, and he moved about among the trees, picking his spots for distance between monitors. He kept a sharp watch for anyone huddled against the all important tree, but no-one looked likely to be Farmer. He had no coherent plan, of course, and there were too many people about for him to hide randomly up a tree, or among bushes. Over and over in his mind he said, I am Ray Burton, I am Ray Burton ... he concentrated on everything that was Burton and tried to forget everything that was Quinn. He let sensations, feelings, atmospheres sink into his Burton awareness, hoping that when he left the park he would remain Burton, and not snap back into darkness.

By dusk he realized that it was hide or take a chance on leaving the park. He decided to take a chance.

As he walked down the slopes, to the pathways, following the crowd, he thought of his arguments with Stormaway, the upsets on board the *Oriel* as they had probed into deep space, the things that had gone wrong, their fears, their anxieties, their awe at Proxima centauri and her belt of planetoids, their anticipation of their return to Earth and ... as he let his mind drift on these things he found a memory coming back ... a memory of trouble on the approach to the Sun ... excitement when Sol was big and bright and the outer solar sphere was just seconds away from their trajectory ... the park gate was getting nearer and Burton tried to slow his pace, but attendants urged him forward and in the bottle-neck at the gate people jostled him faster. He thought rapidly ... trouble, yes, trouble – something wrong as they approached Sol ... they were coming in too fast, much too fast ... he could see Stormaway yelling and Fletcher had his hands over his ears and was screaming words that Burton could not remember ... and Burton was running in panic, and everyone was in a panic ... a green light began to flash angrily, and Sol was getting nearer ...

Darkness.

THREE

WHEN Fabin called later that evening he found Quinn in a very distressed state.

'What could be happening to me, Steve? Am I ill? Do I look ill?'

Fabin shook his head. 'I don't know what's up with you, Andy – confide ... enlighten ...'

Quinn tried to piece his thoughts together. An ambulance passed noisily by outside and he shuddered at the sound of its siren. 'They wouldn't tolerate it – I know they wouldn't. It would be in and in for good. They don't allow mental disorder – hell, Steve, I'm frightened!'

'Tell me what it is. If you don't tell me what's up I can't help at all, can I?'

'I can't, don't you see? I can't tell you. I can't tell anyone.' As if suddenly aware of the ears that might be listening, he shut up and stared at Fabin. Fabin returned his gaze. 'Andy ...' he seemed to be fighting to find the words. 'Andy – I had a call from your office today. You didn't check back to work this afternoon and they've reported you to Employment. They want to know why.'

Quinn's head sank down. 'I suppose they'd be bound to query it. Who else – who else have they contacted?'

Fabin shrugged. 'I expect – well, everyone you know. What happened Andy? Why didn't you go back?'

Quinn said, 'I was in the park. I went in at the usual time – I came out ... you want to know what time I came out? Seven p.m. My God, Steve – *Seven*. I have no idea at all why I was so long. I have no recollection of what I did – Steve, I had a complete blackout.'

Fabin digested that for a moment. 'Okay, so you blacked out. So maybe you're ill, under the weather – that's okay, they can treat that. A few days rest, a week's surveillance—'

Quinn shivered. 'Sure, Steve, sure – like Amis was ill – just a passing depression we all thought – a few days rest, a short course of drugs.'

Fabin had no answering argument. Amis had vanished, thereafter, and it was not hard to guess where. The state did not kill people, it didn't believe in killing, but the reclamation programmes in the U.K. highlands always needed unquestioningly obedient support.

'I'll check in,' said Quinn after a moment. 'In a while. I know I'll have to. But not yet – not for a while.'

Fabin smiled. 'Well, I'll be seeing you, Andy. Take it easy.'

'Sure.'

When Fabin left Quinn turned out the lights and sat in semi-darkness, staring out of his window at the quiet city. He thought over what he had *not* told Fabin, of the false memories he had experienced, a sense of void, of spinning stars and figures, bulky and shapeless but unmistakably men, moving in slow order within the confines of an intricately designed room.

He had remembered being in space, he, Andrew Quinn, who had never achieved the status even to leave the country for a vacation. And space! Memories of space in an age when men were forbidden to think of the stars, and almost forbidden to look towards the Moon.

And who was Burton? Where had he heard the name and why did it seem so significant to him?

Who was Burton?

As if by turning his thoughts to the mystery he had allowed a valve to open, the memories poured back into Quinn's head. For a while he sat motionless, watching the past, listening to the voices of men he had never known. He drank with them, sang with them, flew with them.

And beyond any frontier he had ever conceived of, beyond the stars themselves ... he remembered the trials and frustrations of the months long flight, the agony of the discovery that there were no habitable worlds around their destination star. The return flight, and the anger flaring, the fist fights, the long silences . . . and thus up against the blank wall, the approach to Earth, the moment when memory stopped . . .

By the time the fever of recollection had passed away and whoever or whatever lay within his head had become quiet for a while, Quinn was trembling violently. He felt a great sadness, and his own life seemed to recollect itself to him, confronting him with the little he had done in thirty years, marching past him as if for the last time.

He experienced a sense of finality. Burton – it *was* a man called Burton wasn't it? – was moving him out. He became aware of the ever present subliminal barrage, the voice of the country, dictating his mood, his behaviour. It was no longer having an effect. Quinn was beyond control, and the presence from below his mind's surface was a stronger man than he.

These were Quinn's last few minutes alive, and he wanted desperately to cry. But he sank down, submerged beneath the hubbub of an alien life, and quietly passed into death.

It was midnight.

Burton watched the sleeping city and felt triumphant. He had fought hard to regain awareness and, whilst he felt sorry for his host, it was more important to Burton that a man called Burton was alive rather than a stranger called Andrew Quinn.

Quickly, then, he examined the room. It was small and functional, a microcosm of late twenty-third century culture. One wall, however, was covered with photographs taken towards the end of the twentieth century, of cities and people or was the twentieth century the age of narcissism, and the only age to develop a photographic culture?

The kitchen was well stocked and Burton cooked fresh fish and butter beans. As the meal was preparing – it took just over a minute – he scrutinized the rest of the apartment.

The coffin enclosure he was expecting; but it was still a shock. Seven mummies, all perfectly preserved, but showing just sufficient signs of death to present as macabre. Burton shut them away hastily.

He ate his meal and settled down to think.

He was free, that was one thing; but from what he could

gather by his difficult eavesdropping on the life of Andrew Quinn, Quinn had now made himself known to the authorities. And that meant, Burton was almost sure, that he would be in trouble. Either he could run, try and hide and set about finding Stormaway surreptitiously, or he could brazen it out, admit to what he had done – as Quinn – and hope for an instant reprimand and nothing more.

Whatever he chose to do as regarded Quinn's aberrations, he had to find Stormaway. And he had to hope that Stormaway was now on the surface too, since he could not try and find him in the park. That would be far too dangerous.

So, find Stormaway. But then what?

Although it was unclear to Burton what he would *do* next, at the back of his mind, and pushing ever forward, was the question: what happened after we came within spitting distance of Earth? There was just a blank. A horrifyingly complete blank. And in the time that that blank covered somehow he and Stormaway, and perhaps the four others, had become imprisoned in the bodies – and minds – of ordinary citizens.

Who had done the imprisoning?

At that moment something in the room called for attention with a low but penetrating buzz.

It took just a moment to recognize the source of sound as the small screen above Quinn's correspondence desk, and Burton crossed the room, played for a few seconds and then managed to open the visual circuit. A man's face stared out at him, searched his eyes for a moment – just a moment – and then said, 'Mr. Quinn?

Burton had seen the man before, but his memory failed him as he reacted quickly and uncertainly to the unexpected contact.

'That's right,' he said. 'And you are?'

'Department of Health . . .' At midnight? Burton was instantly suspicious. As if reading his thoughts, or perhaps the unconscious puzzlement that expressed itself on Burton's face, the man went on, 'We work round the clock, like most government departments. You should know that Mr. Quinn. Or perhaps you didn't. That's only a detail among details. What is important is that you make immediate contact with the department of Employment at KET2549–410 and explain your failure to return to work this afternoon. It's very important, Mr. Quinn, that you do that. Explain that you were dizzy and stayed in the park for safety. Will you do that Mr. Quinn?'

'Yes,' said Burton flatly. Mention of the park had jogged his memory. This was the man he had seen watching him on one occasion. It was unmistakably the same man.

'That way, Mr. Quinn,' said the man on the screen, 'your transgression can be logged routine, and the Employment-offences will get back to you in about four weeks. Understand?'

'Yes, I believe I do ... I had been about to report in, anyway. Thank you.'

'You're welcome. Oh, and Mr. Quinn. Are you fully *recovered*?'

'I've come right through, yes. Thank you again.'

'Excellent.'

The image faded and Burton cut the circuit. He recharged the screen and dialled the number he had been given. He got through to a recording system and stated his report flatly, and briefly, and rang off.

Unless he was being duped, he had four weeks before he would fall foul of an investigation. And if he wasn't being duped, the man who had just spoken to him was someone he could trust, and who knew enough to help him.

The following day Burton checked into Quinn's place of work and sat down behind his desk. Nobody seemed to pay much attention to him, although one man came up to him and asked him how he felt.

'Fine,' said Burton. 'Top of the world.'

'That's more like it,' said the other man. 'I'll see you for a drink later. Okay?'

Burton nodded and smiled and the other man walked off, leaving Burton facing the least of his problems. What the hell did Quinn do with the sheets of symbols and statistics piled on his desk, and the various screens and typewriter consoles that surrounded him?

There were two other men in the same office, and they possessed the same set-up as Quinn. All morning they typed, swore, spent long minutes in silence, scratching on paper occasionally, and then back to the typewriter, or computer input key, and a frantic burst of activity. Burton aped the action, and spent a boring and strenuous morning.

At 12.30 the man sitting across the room from him closed down the humming machinery that surrounded him and rose. 'You coming to lunch, Andy? Peter?'

At last, thought Burton. And aloud; 'Not today. Some shopping to do.'

The other two men seemed surprised. The one called Peter said: 'You wangled a pass card from the building? You lucky dog. I was refused one only yesterday.'

That was a blow for Burton. He desperately wanted to get out of the building and take a look around. But when he checked at the entrance of the office block he was not allowed access to the street outside. Two female guards, paunchy and uninterested, turned him away, but pointed out that the Director was in a good mood and might vouchsafe a permit if he was humble.

Burton walked back towards his office, passing, as he did so, a private holophone booth. There were directories inside and he took the opportunity to locate Dan Farmer. He lived two miles north of where Quinn lived, in a block of flats in Stamford.

He arrived home shortly after six, and checked out an hour later. He went straight to where Farmer lived and rang the bell of the man's flat. After a moment the door opened and Farmer stood there, a meagre looking man, but tall and with an air of strength. He also had a slightly indulgent look about him, and yet, from Stormaway's description in the diary, he was a man of few indulgences.

'Yes?'

'Are you ... Stormaway?'

Whatever Burton had expected, he had not anticipated the violence of the man's response. Incomprehension, Burton had half expected; a welcoming handclasp he had hoped for.

Farmer grabbed him by the neck and dragged him into the room, throwing him across the floor with a screech almost animal in its intensity.

Dazed and confused Burton struggled to his feet, only to

feel himself thrown against the wall, there to be held by very powerful hands.

Farmer was blazing red. His face was contorted with an emotion Burton imagined was rage. But it could have been fear – deep seated, soul destroying fear.

'What's happening to me?' screamed Farmer. 'Who the hell is Stormaway and why is he plaguing me? Who is he?'

Burton tried to extricate himself from the grip, but Quinn's body was not strong. Farmer hit him in the mouth and tripped him over, throwing him to the ground.

'Farmer, for God's sake, cool down . . .'

'Who's Stormaway?' screamed Farmer by way of response. He came down on Burton with the weight of his body directed through his knees. Burton's breath went from him and he began to feel sick. He noticed that Farmer was crying. 'For God's sake what's happening to me? *What's happening to me?* Who is this man who's . . . who's always in my head? Oh God, what's happening?'

He began to weep and Burton, feeling weak and shaken, summoned the strength to throw him off his body. Farmer immediately began to struggle to his feet, but Burton was quicker. He aimed a kick at Farmer's head, and connected perfectly. Farmer went sprawling.

As he subsided against the far wall, blood gushing from his nose, so Burton ran for the door. He was obviously too early. As he left the apartment, however, he paused, looked back at Farmer who was trying to sit up. He was saying something, a name . . . Burton's name . . . just once, he said it, and then collapsed backwards.

Burton came back into the room and knelt above the semi-conscious figure. The lips were moving, almost with difficulty.

'Stormaway, it's me . . . can you hear me?'

'Can't . . . get through, Ray . . . but fighting . . . give me time . . . a little time . . . hell, I'm sinking . . . tomorrow . . . park . . .'

He said nothing more, but Farmer began to regain consciousness, moaning and wiping a hand across his blood stained face.

Burton took his leave.

The following day Burton made a decision that was. guessed, almost certainly a mistake. But if Burton had flaw at all it was that he was impatient, and he could wait for Stormaway to make the breakthrough on his ow He would have to do as Stormaway had suggested and mee him in the park.

To meet him in the park meant either getting an ex permit from his place of work, and hoping he could get into the park unnoticed, or not going into work at all. He chose the latter course.

Towards mid-day he joined the long queue shuffling into the wide expanse of the park. As he passed through the gates so, like everyone else, he flashed his small identity card at the television monitor on the right. So now the fact that he was in the park at an illegal time would be made known to the authorities. But how long would it take for them to react? He knew, from his *own* experience, that no such identification was made at the exit. With luck, then, they would try and catch up with him at home. And he had no intention of going home, not until he had a clear plan of action amenable to both himself and Stormaway.

He made straight for the oak, but no-one was there, so he sat down and waited, reading through the diary interchange many times while the minutes ticked by.

Two hours later he noticed a man running and walking towards him, a man conspicuous by his lack of calm.

As he drew nearer Burton recognized Farmer, now with his nose covered in plaster. As Farmer drew near he hesitated, staring at Burton as if searching for a sign that he had the right man. He said: 'I don't recognize you . . .'

'I'm Burton.'

'Ray. My God, is it really you?'

They shook hands, staring at the alien forms that contained their souls. 'Quite a come down from the muscle perfect bodies we started with, eh? You're weedy, I'm running to fat in all the wrong places.'

They sat down. Inevitably for a while there was silence. Then Stormaway said: 'How'd you break through?'

n said: 'It happened two nights back. Almost nat-
. Quinn was a very weak man, totally ruled by what-
rules people in this society. He was a characterless man.
as inevitable that he should succumb; but when it hap-
ed I was quite surprised. What had been a persisting
yness, a dream-like awareness of what he was seeing and
ng, suddenly became hard reality.'

Stormaway thought about that for a moment. 'A trigger
erhaps. A delayed response. I haven't broken through yet;
ut I've felt my power increasing and my host has obviously
been becoming very uptight.'

'Has he drawn attention to himself yet?'

'Only last night when you called. No, I think he's okay.
He's kept his blackouts to himself, as far as I can discern. I
feel the greyness subsiding, as you just described. It can only
be a matter of time.'

'You said a delayed action. Does that mean you have an
idea?'

Stormaway nodded. 'Nothing particularly rational. But as
you will have noticed, the most blatant feature of this
society is its intolerances. I suppose all societies have them,
but here we have a government that has banned any con-
course with space; no space travel, and it ought to be commonplace. No records in public places of the space flight
achievements of the past. At least, none that I can discern.'

'They also seem intolerant of non-Christian thinking.'

'Precisely so,' said Stormaway. He leaned back against the
sturdy oak and let his gaze wander among the people
around about. 'They're a very God fearing nation, and no
doubt about it. Unless I'm much mistaken they place great
importance on everything that in our day on Earth was regarded as Christian fiction – angels, judgment day, battles
between good and evil.'

And that, thought Burton, might account for the degree of
militancy the society displayed. There was no reason,
Burton knew, why militancy and Christianity shouldn't
mix, after all, Christianity was the militant among Earth's
religions, and had obviously – by all the signs – proved the
policy was successful. And it would not be hard to justify
the use of subversive techniques in a society that was obviously functioning and content.

Burton said, 'Assuming a phobia concerning all things off-worldly, an irrational fear that leaving Earth was against God's wishes, or that—' he remembered the picture in Quinn's apartment – 'space was the territory of the forces of evil, how would such a society treat a returning space-farer? And there must be many of them.'

Stormaway stroked his bruised cheek. 'I imagine they would suppress such returning heroes. And I imagine that, since they would have no interest in what they know, they would kill them.'

Burton couldn't help but agree in principle. 'They don't, apparently, kill people in this society. But since we don't belong . . . perhaps the same ethical code would not be applicable to treatment of living fossils.'

'We're not living fossils and we're far from dead. We've just misplaced our bodies . . .' they looked at each other. 'There was no technology of mind transplant when we left was there?'

'Not that I remember,' said Burton. 'But we were away long enough for it to be developed . . . and if it was developed, and was used on us . . .'

'Then,' concluded Stormaway. 'Someone saved us, saved what we know. If we're right in what we surmise, then it could be that our own minds were suppressed for a few months, perhaps years, until such a time as our arrival was well in the past, and the ruling forces were merely anxious about the next ship that might return home at any moment. At such a safe time we begin to return to awareness, and perhaps our hosts were selected for weaknesses of personality to aid our return, although I wish they'd been a little more selective when it came to selecting someone for me . . .'

Burton said, 'I had a call two nights ago from a man I saw watching me one day.'

'Did he see the diary?'

'Not as far as I know. He warned me that a time I delayed leaving the park would catch up with me quickly unless I owned up, in which case it would be a routine chastisement some weeks hence. He's the key, Stormaway. He may only be a pawn, but he's the key to who helped us, and we need those people now.'

'I agree. But how to find him?'

After a long think, a period of silence during which they became abruptly aware they would have to be moving off, Burton said: 'Let's take a chance and hope he'll find *us*. I don't see what else we can do.'

Unwilling to take more risks – and the very uncertainty of whether or not he was taking risks at all was an unnerving experience on its own – Burton made straight for Farmer's flat. He spent the afternoon crouched in the darkest place he could find, which was in a small, doorless cupboard beneath the stairs, one flight of steps above Farmer's apartment.

When he heard Farmer arrive home after work, he walked quietly down to where the man was fumbling with the keys of the admission panel, and as the door opened and Farmer made to go inside, Burton pushed him hard and came into the flat after him.

Farmer shouted loudly with surprise and spun round, fists clenched. When he saw Burton he said, 'You again. What the hell do you want?'

'I can help,' said Burton quickly. 'I mean it. I can help. Just keep calm.'

Farmer visibly relaxed and walked round Burton to close the door and lock it. 'They used to keep us happy,' he said. 'I didn't know it until yesterday, but they used to keep us happy. They still do, I suppose. All the time, a constant barrage of cheerfulness; mood control. Frightening isn't it. When it stopped working for me I began to realize what a handsome little puppet I'd been all these years. I *am* calm, mister; I'm very calm. I blacked out today when I went into the park. I obviously did something because I walked in and walked out fully aware. But I'm calm about it. If I keep quiet, if I don't make a fuss, maybe it'll pass away. Maybe Stormaway will stop haunting me . . . whoever the hell he is. And maybe . . . maybe you'll stop bothering me, whoever the hell you are.'

'My name's Burton.'

Farmer nodded. He walked to a small cabinet and opened it. There was a comprehensive range of drinks within it and he squeezed himself a shot of rum. 'I always had a well stocked drinks cabinet, Mister Burton, but I never ever touched it. For my friends only. A few days ago I began to get a great longing for rum.' He looked at Burton. 'I'm pretty sure I know why, and I'd fight it. But I rather like the stuff, now, so I'll concede him that point.' He paused, stared at Burton as if searching for some confirmation of what he was thinking. After a moment he said, 'I'm going to offer you a drink. I was hysterical yesterday, and although you used foul means whereas I'd used only fair, I nevertheless feel I owe you an apology. What'll you have?'

'I'll take the rum. Thanks.'

Farmer squeezed the shot and emptied the dispenser. He passed the glass to Burton and raised his own to the level of his eyes, glanced at it and drank its contents in a single swallow.

'So, Mister Burton – how can you help me?'

Burton stared at the man. He was so relaxed, so determined, that Burton realized he had no ploy to make. Or had he? He said, 'I wanted to urge you to total calm, but I see you are relaxed already. I'm mistaken, I can't help you.'

'Why did you want to urge me to total calm?'

'Because what you're going through, I went through.'

Farmer seemed surprised. 'And just what am I going through, Mister Burton?'

'You're being taken over. And from your behaviour last night, I'd say he was doing well.'

Farmer paled. He stared at his empty glass, then placed it carefully on the arm of his chair. 'You were being taken over?'

Burton nodded.

'And you resisted and won?'

'Yes,' Burton lied. 'It was hard, but I found that resistance merely assisted the taking over. It strengthened the process of invasion. I relaxed, filled my mind with myself, and resisted the forces within me. While I was fighting I found out there was a link between what was inside me and what was inside a man called Farmer. That's why I knew of you.'

Farmer stared at him, unblinking, confident. 'You relaxed and you won.' Burton affirmed. Farmer said: 'There are too many questions to ask even a single one, yet, but I trust you, Burton. When I've won my battle we'll find out what's been happening to us. Won't we?'

Burton affirmed again. 'I'm determined to.'

After a moment Farmer reached across and extended his hand. Burton shook it. He felt just slightly cheap.

They drank some more, but talked little. Farmer was making a visible effort to relax, little realizing that Stormaway would now be able to make his pressure count. By mid-evening, in the dimly lit apartment, with no sound penetrating from outside and only the rhythm of their breathing disturbing the stillness inside, Farmer began to fade.

'I'm losing, Burton,' he said. His eyes opened and he turned his head to look at the other man. There was a question in his eyes, and the answer was on Burton's face. 'You bastard,' said Farmer softly. 'Oh God . . . oh dear God, I'm a dead man . . .'

The holophone screen màde noises at midnight. When Stormaway activated it he found himself looking at the man from the department of Health. 'Is Quinn there?'

'Sure,' said Stormaway and moved aside as Burton positioned himself before the small screen.

The man looking at him said: 'Your colleague, Farmer, looks under the weather – will he pull through?'

'He already has,' said Burton. 'He's much better, thanks.'

'Excellent. Do you have a nightwalk permit for tonight?' Burton shook his head. 'I thought not. Stay with Farmer tonight and make sure he doesn't . . . relapse. I think the L and O department will allow me to donate you that small transgression. In the morning *do* make an effort to go to work. We have your case in this department and the Employment offences bureau is waiting for our report before taking action, so really you have nothing to worry about. Leave at exactly 9.30 and walk to your apartment, and then to work. Is that clear?'

Burton nodded.

'Put Farmer back on, will you? Farmer? Don't overdo it. Keep absolutely clean and we'll try and make sure we give you a good report. Your blackouts are, unfortunately, known to us, but we do understand. Leave for work at exactly 9.45 tomorrow morning. Is that clear?'

'Yes. Thankyou.'

The screen faded. Stormaway said: 'Can you trust him?'

'If not him, then no one. He has to be careful what he says, but his message gets through loud and clear. I think he's been waiting for both of us to break through before taking positive action. Now I think we'll see the things move ahead.'

'We don't really have much choice, I suppose. But I'd still like to know what happened to the other four of us.'

'He may be able to tell us,' said Burton. 'Until then, there's no point in worrying about it.'

They made themselves at home in Dan Farmer's fairly luxurious apartment, and made good progress with his drinks cabinet. Then they exhausted themselves, remembering old times, and slept soundly until sunrise.

FIVE

AT THE specified time Burton slipped from Farmer's flat and made his way out into the street. He began to walk briskly towards his apartment, over two miles away.

After a few minutes walking a figure matched velocity and said, 'Slow down, Burton, there's no rush.'

Burton slowed and glanced sideways. He saw who he expected to see, the man who had become his link with hope. He was short, shorter than Burton remembered him from the time in the park. He smiled at Burton and passed him an envelope. Burton hesitated before taking it.

'We're in a blind zone for ten yards, and in a five percent audio zone for twenty. Nobody is going to bother filtering out our conversation at that sort of level.'

'Thanks. I feel very insecure—'

'Anticipated.' The man smiled. 'The one vice of your century that has hung over into ours is an addiction to listening and watching, but it's very easy to discover the weak points in the system. I've given you brief instructions and a night pass for tonight. Stay cool, eh? Stay on the right side of the law.'

'I will.'

Five paces left in the deaf zone.

'Your future is, I'm afraid, not one I'd bet on.'

'I understand that.'

'But if you keep your head we'll at least get some information from you.'

Burton nodded, feeling a chill creeping through him. He said: 'What about the others? There were four others . . .'

'Alive and well. Don't worry . . .'

He was gone, then, and Burton kept walking towards his apartment. Once in the fairly assured security of his room he looked at the instructions. A location at which he would be met. If there was no one waiting for him there he was to keep walking without looking about him and return at length to his room, there to await further instructions.

There was something attractively melodramatic about the situation, but something horribly persistant about the tension in his stomach.

During the long day the tension ebbed and the reality – the saddening reality – of the situation caught up with Burton once more.

He least of all had expected a hero's return. Stormaway and Pearson had been those with dreams of glory; as men returning from the stars they would become cultural artifacts in their own right, adored and adorned, idolized and remembered through time. Burton had had no such delusions. To begin with, yes, he had dreamed of what lay ahead, planned along with the best of them. But he went into space as part of his job and he had come to find the dreams of his two colleagues unbearably naïve; that had sparked the trouble and the hostility, and the trip had only just begun. There had been three others who had remained fairly neutral, and formed a group as of their own, and thus Burton had found himself alone with his thoughts for much of the tedious flight towards Proxima C.

In the days of exploration that followed there had been no men with dreams, only machines scrutinizing every inch of space, scanning every orbit for signs of a planetary existence.

But Proxima C. was a sun without a planet larger than the

moon of Earth, and of those it had many thousands, spread through a volume of space twenty light minutes in radius. There had been no life on any of them, and no possibility of colonization.

That had been heartbreaking to the dreamers, cold fact, but disappointing none the less, to Burton. They sent what they had found back to Earth, seventeen minutes of compressed information, repeated one hundred times. They had debated what to do next, return to Earth and face the adjustments to a time nearly three centuries in advance of their own era, or move outwards, outwards for the rest of their natural lifespans, supported by the near endless supplies on board the ship.

The majority vote had been to return, only Burton and one other voting to continue.

And the journey back, the months of bad feeling, growing and growing, sparking into spontaneous rows, precipitating terrible fights in the confines of the ship. Burton's banishment to cold space for seven days, then Pearson's, figures spiralling in the void, foodless, sobbing and shrieking, aware of the watching faces from the lighted window just yards away, and the stars moving in slow circles and the sense of time passing . . .

With what they had done and what they had been through, they had returned to Earth. And instead of heroes, instead of artifacts, instead, even, of fossils, they had become . . . nothing. They were not wanted, they were not sought for. Rather, they seemed to have been hidden away from the human eye of the 23rd century after Christ.

In a sense, however, what had happened had given Burton a fresh incentive to live. He had not been a man after glory, as Stormaway had been. He had wanted to regurgitate his feelings and observations, and live, then, in the secure knowledge that he had contributed something to the progress of man. But he returned to find that if he was to contribute anything at all it was to be to a movement that existed out of sight and out of hearing of the ruling forces, that he was the great incentive for an underground that had rescued his mind and could therefore learn again of the stars and how to reach them. His experience would not be lost, although it would be a long, long time, Burton was sure, before common sense and a desire for progress returned to the country.

And perhaps – he realized he had never found out – to the whole wide world?

But then what? What was his future when he had told what he knew? It was a depressing thought. He would have to make the adjustment to being Andrew Quinn, learning his trade and his weaknesses, his past and his destiny. Aware that the slightest mistake, the most insignificant incongruity, could mean his end. As the man had said, Burton's was not a future to put money on.

Burton opened his eyes and stared up at a white ceiling unbroken by even a single crack. For a moment he was confused. He had been walking to the appointed place at the appointed time; he had been met by a middle aged woman, and they had begun to walk back the way he had just come . . .

'How do you feel Burton?'

That voice. The link man – and Burton knew his name: Keiran Moran.

Moran came into Burton's field of vision and stared down at him, his face seeming stark and frightening in the harsh light of the room.

'How do you feel?'

In the instant that Moran repeated his question, full recollection of events distant and recent formed in Burton's mind. He felt a great wave of relief pass through him and felt no concern when two strange faces appeared above him, standing on the other side of his body to Moran. They both looked down at him with a professionally detached air. Moran was saying, 'Everything come back to you?'

Yes, thought Burton. Who, he wondered, had miscalculated the moment to initiate deceleration? Who – and it had not been him – had tried to decelerate so rapidly on Earth approach that the protective mechanisms in the ship had gone haywire and caused such panic? He could remember trying, and failing, to switch over to auto-control, and Stormaway crawling across his helpless body and reaching the vital switch. And the next thing he knew had been this same room, with awareness of a barrage of questions and his arms and legs punctured a million times by needles thin and thick.

'There is no time for anything,' a voice – Moran's? – had said to him. 'They want to see your bodies and we have to work fast. When you recover you may feel confused, memory may not be complete; we've made your special tree in the open-park at Hammersmith an enhancing trigger and it should help full recovery. We'll find out everything when the heat is off. The other four we're keeping alive for a while – you and Stormaway were both injured on landing.'

That had been all.

Moran said, now, 'Is everything clear to you? Has it all come back?'

'Yes,' said Burton. 'In retrospect it would have been one hell of a coincidence both myself and Stormaway managing to make contact in the way we did.'

'The tree and the diary, you mean. The diary was an unexpected development. We had to fix it so that Stormaway found the book, but it was a useful development. What *was* a coincidence was that that particular tree was virtually in a blind spot. That was convenient.'

Burton struggled to sit up, but he felt restrained and collapsed backwards, feeling dizzy.

'Relax,' said Moran. He looked over at one of the two men who still watched Burton silently. From the very corner of his eye Burton saw the man administer an injection to his right upper arm. Moran went on, 'We had not realized the extent to which memory would lag behind awareness in the recovery process, nor that having triggered your recovery on entry into the park, the park itself would become a strong signal, and leaving the park a signal to become lost again. We think you may have been right – or was it Stormaway? – when you said that the lessened subliminal barrage in the area may have been an important factor. We hadn't taken that into account.

'Not to worry. Everything went off splendidly. And we have a full account from you both, taken a few minutes ago.'

'Good' Burton could still remember nothing from the moment he had been met and brought to a tumble down,

21st century house, standing in its own small allotment, and then being put into drug induced hypnosis.

Perhaps seeing his dissatisfaction, Moran spoke a series of numbers and the full debriefing recollected itself to Burton.

Immediately he was confused.

'I can't help remembering,' he said, 'That you asked me nothing about my time in space or of what I know of the technology of space travel. All you asked me about was ... my recovery ...'

Moran smiled. 'You must appreciate, Burton, that this is the first time we have experimented with personality and memory transplant. It's a difficult technology to develop because it is not approved ...'

'I understand that,' said Burton. 'But surely, if our futures are as insecure as you say, then shouldn't you get as much information concerning the technology of space as you can?'

There was a moment's silence during which Moran and Burton exchanged an unbroken stare. 'Burton, you will be aware by now that the transplant of what is essentially a human being from one body to another can only be accomplished with the death of the donor. That's why you died. And why you could never go back into your old body.

'When we began to plan the infiltration of higher offices of government we knew we had to come up with a technique that was new, that would not be anticipated. Listening devices were out, and so were spies of any description. Brainwashing or hypnotic conditioning of established personnel was out because the first technique takes too long, and the second – well, hypnotic programmes can be broken at a distance of ten miles.

'We conceived of this: a delayed action transplant of one of our number into a high official of state. But how to research and develop the technique? We couldn't just pluck a man from the street and kill him in a trial run. Nobody is executed any more, and besides, that would be monitored – and people dying in hospitals are monitored unto the bitter end.

'When we came up with the idea, and developed the basic technology, we realized we had come up against a void that we could not cross. Until one day – out of the literal blue – came six embarrassments to the government.

'Because of what you were and what you represented you could not be allowed to live. No way. And who got the job of disposal? The department of Health of course, the easiest department to infiltrate at the lower levels, and it was to the lower levels that the dirty work was donated. With a great blind eye turned to what we did.

'Suddenly, Burton, three months ago – yes, only three months – we had our experimental donors. No, don't try and move. What you've received is not the sort of paralytic agent to be argued with.

'Six donors, Burton. All to ourselves. We used two in the first test, and by all the signs, from everything you say, we will only have to do one or two more. And we still have four guinea pigs to choose from.

'By your eyes I think you're fading, Burton, but as you sink into the sort of sleep you never dreamed existed, let me assure you that when this country resumes its common sense, when better men – and women – sit in power and judgment over this island, your sacrifice will not be forgotten. Quinn, of course, is not dead and he must be returned and the events of the past weeks eliminated from him. We'd let *you* live, but . . . well, the danger you represent to this government you'd also represent to ours. If nothing else we're good Churchmen, Burton, and if we don't like mass subversion, that's one thing – but we have no intention of opening our arms to the forces of evil.'

THE GREAT PLAN

by

Leroy Kettle

Most sensible people do not have enough time to be bored. Most sensible people would think to pack more than one wine-bird. But, as Leroy Kettle (revere) who is noted for the cunning quality of his humour, here points out, boredom, the work ethic and sense are inextricably mixed. Perhaps the True Tragedie was that for Burgundal and his cronies, meaning itself had lost meaning ...

THE GREAT PLAN

BURGUNDAL laughed in the light, wide way which indicated extreme delight. It was luze-whispering time, as always when the year was so far through, and he had just formulated the Great Plan, which gave all appearances of being a splendid diversion. Because of these things there was more goodness in the soft, warm air than usual. Burgundal, not necessarily a person to whom goodness meant anything special, was actually savouring the experience and storing it for possible future recollection. His cheeks, below their amusing gold whorls, flushed with what should perhaps be called ecstasy while the ancient sign affixed to his high forehead flashed COKE in wild, red abandon. Even his hair seemed to be more restless than usual.

The days passed quickly as he sat on the realistically gnarled branches mumbling happily to the fruit; but, eventually, the slight tension in the brain he used most often, caused by his thoughts of the Great Plan, forced him to relinquish the primitive though exhilarating company of the luze, and act.

When he judged the moment to be appropriate and the tone-winds were strong, he yelled good and loud within his mind. Somewhere, and in other places, people heard him. He waited just a short time to ensure they were the right people, as tradition decreed (though there were only right people to hear), then, no longer tense, and with a mild excitement in his secondary voice, he whispered to the luze and learned a little, taught a little.

Some while later those same right people gathered together in their hundreds at the great desk of Burgundal within the largest, most comfortable, most hard to leave room, not only in his Tuesday Palace but probably above, below, and upon the whole of that particular land area. The caller himself was not yet present and speculation was rife as to the reason for the calling.

Undlum, a Man of unreasonable height, young enough to assume iridescent bones and kaleidoscope eyes, but old enough to be listened to (or, at least, heard) suggested it was from pure joy that Burgundal had shouted.

'For are his eccentricities not well-known? And what is more eccentric, and thus to him more pleasurable, in these times than a call?' Greatly satisfied with his contribution to the discussion, Undlum ate of the grapes which briefly grew by him.

However, Callastop, that erstwhile student of Human deviousness, too old to be other than wry and cynical, said: 'Burgundal is rarely capable of performing anything merely joyously and certainly not with purity. He has, and always will have, himself solely as the centre of whatever thoughts spin between his brains. Not precisely a fit subject for one day's contemplation, let alone an eternity. His mind butterflies around and he thinks all should stop to admire its pretty colours. But the intellectual capacity of a peacock is not noticeably increased when it spreads its tail.'

Callastop had undertaken her primary establishment during a period of fashionable austerity and it showed in her drabness of dress and appreciation, her long, plain-silver hair, and her meagre anatomical embellishments. She also failed to notice, or respond to, Undlum's obvious dismay made most apparent by his dimmed skeletal structure.

She continued, 'He has probably called for no reason, or perhaps to demonstrate his latest fazm. Silly, dry, little thing.'

There were loud murmurs of 'Never' and 'Could well be', until the oldest, and wisest when all went well, of those gathered, shifted on his velvet and warm-ice couch, and said: 'Pooh.'

Magrib was renowned for his perception and so all were quiet, though the sag could detect some uncompliments about Burgundal drifting by. Once, even, though he felt too slowly to tell from where, the tone-wind carried the description of a surgically strenuous operation which would enable Burgundal to return to the more horizontal orders of the animal kingdom from whence he had undoubtably arrived in error. The small, wrinkled appearance adopted by the philosopher became more small and wrinkled as his annoyance increased but that soon departed as it was one of the more base feelings. If some other chose to interest himself in rudeness, that was really no concern of Magrib's. Everyone was free. He had thought, in his unusual fit of pique, to leave and return to study the rather ancient mountain he had recently found existed in his favourite retreat; but, as these trifling upsets should not control him, he remained.

At last, and with no apologies, Burgundal arrived. One second he was not there and the next he was only just there and the next he had some substance, until, after many such seconds, he appeared solidly and actually before them. There was a little disappointment, even from his detractors, that he had not descended upon them in an inventively pyrotechnical manner, and without luze leaves and cobwebs on his immaculately reconstructed, old-time, green smock.

He stood there, tall and broad, before the vast expanse of intricately carved desk, and looked around between the towering, pure-white pillars which supported the recently added flicker-beam roof. There sat, lay or aired the whole of True Humanity, friends and unfriends. He knew their disappointment and regretted his rather arrogant dismissal of the need for a grand entry, until he spoke. They were not disappointed then.

'I,' he announced in a fine, powerful voice, 'have formulated the Great Plan.'

Gasps of amazement came from all parts of the room in a fashion exceeding ritual demand.

'The Great Plan,' echoed some of the True Humans, tasting the words, sucking their significance dry.

The words shone upon Burgundal's lips and dripped like the very best honey from his tongue. They resounded from the ivory walls as had Vaffly's Horn of Triumph in the days of the First Separation, but were also as soft as the cry of a silarg. It was a glorious moment.

Finally, well-satisfied with the reaction despite his feeling that some present had only registered token astonishment, Burgundal raised a jewel-encrusted hand.

'Cease,' he commanded, exercising temporary ascendancy by virtue of the call. Gradually the mutterings and tonings came to a halt.

'We, True Humanity, are met together at my request so that we may all share in the glory of my Great Plan. I trust you will be so kind as to allow me the honour of describing its workings.'

Callastop looked at her friends and they nodded among themselves. Perong's undemonstrative, self-aware faction also nodded. Other groups, and individuals with no usual desire or ability to join in shared amusements (perhaps it was their quiet time), also nodded, with the exception of Magrib, who may or may not have inclined his head. There did indeed seem to be a general concensus that Burgundal should continue.

He reached for the crystal goblet which forever floated at his side, and filled it from a passing wine-bird. He drank deeply of the nectar, spilling a little which dissolved in the ingeniously tidy air. The others emulated him depending on their proximity to a wine-bird; the poor creatures were always at a loss when uncommon interest was shown in their produce. Burgundal let the fire of the drink burn along his veins. He waved his goblet in an all-inclusive, though somewhat dampening, gesture.

'Here we have everything we may wish for,' he said in as serious a voice as he possessed. 'We live easily on this, our home planet. Our long ago and good Ancestors (revere their names) provided us with the means to live with scarcely the need for a thought let alone a physical action unless we ourselves are desirous of such. We have separated from the mundane galaxy over which we once held sway, and we exist solely for ourselves, to be the centre of our own galaxies of thought.'

Here Callastop had the grace to blush a very little, though she felt she ought to be outraged.

'The castles of our minds,' (Burgundal's metaphors were not the most consistent), 'have for their walls stupendous talents. Some of us choose to lie in the shadows of these walls, others attempt to climb them. Perhaps too many are not among the strugglers to the summit.'

He looked around darkly. Most of the True Humans found they could not meet his gaze. It was mostly a small trick he performed with concealed mirrors.

'There seems to be nothing we lack. Or is there?'

He paused, and in that pause Magrib said something very quietly.

'Ah, Magrib, ancient delver into reason,' (for Burgundal had heard, not being so totally involved in his own mind as some might suggest) 'has age deadened your voice?'

Magrib, openly derisive of attention-attracting effects, merely spoke in reply, making no attempt at physical or mental gaudiness. 'Don't be too clever there, Burgundal. Not too clever.'

He sipped his wine from an ebony chalice, allowing time to rush on without him, demonstrating his disregard for haste. His old, grey lips smacked with pleasure as he wiped blatantly at his green-streaked beard.

'I will tell you what you wish to hear. We lack purpose.'

Burgundal immediately resumed his speech having become impatient with the aged Human's slightly hypocritical stage-stealing, and he missed (or did he choose to ignore?) Magrib's final words. 'But do we need it?'

Burgundal shouted, 'Exactly. Purpose. We lack purpose.'

He surveyed the audience quickly and discreetly, assessing their mostly silent response to his utterance. He seemed to have them, including Callastop and friends. There was no hostility, nothing even so tenuous as a raised eyebrow.

'If we could do something which was great and good and always remembered, would not that make it all worthwhile?'

'What is there to make worthwhile?' inquired Callastop, uncertain as to the intended destination of Burgundal's line of logic but not wishing him to have any easy route there.

Burgundal frowned. He thought for a moment while he set his face in a look of contemptuous superiority. Not wishing his diversion to be concluded so soon, he found the right defence to Callastop's unexpectedly direct inquiry.

'How can you, of all True Humanity, ask such a question? Surely it is you who are the most vocal critic whenever we appear to be more self-indulgent than normal. I cannot believe that when I offer you a chance to make your life, and help in making all our lives, worthy of the great trust placed there by our Ancestors (revere) you would spurn me.

'We have lived selfish, wastrel existences long enough. If we are to continue in this fashion we must perform an act of unparalleled generosity in order that we may keep faith with the past. Then we can live once more as we choose, but in the knowledge that we have left a mark on the galaxy, that we are not a meaningless few, that the Great Human who created all will not despise us.

'Is this not so?'

'Yes,' said some, dubiously. And, after a moment, 'YES,' said many as the fire from the speech and the wine touched them and Burgundal played ever so gently with their minds. Even Callastop said: 'Yes,' but she was not sure why. Magrib shook his head.

Burgundal flashed his decorative COKE sign. 'Here is what I plan,' he said.

Every Human leaned forward, or at least lounged less freely. They had not experienced such group anticipation since awaiting the ironic climax of Trippolino's Hundred Year Suicide at some distant time past.

'We are the last on Earth,' said Burgundal, his hands flashing in demonstrative gestures, as he was more intoxicated with his rhetoric than with the wine. 'We are the direct descendants of the first, True Humanity. Those lower forms of man, also descended from our Ancestor's (revere, revere) ancestors, but by a devious, far from pure, route, have spread throughout the galaxy. They were not among the elite whose intellects were thought worth improving, pampering, eternalizing. However, somewhere deep inside, I am sure you realize, they are our brothers and sisters.'

Many were the sounds of amazement at this effrontery. Why, everyone knew that only True Humans had been saved at the First Separation, and then undertook self-isolation when the barbaric hordes elsewhere in the galaxy would not leave them alone. The hoi-polloi were rather agitated, it appeared, that so much in the way of *their* raw materials had been utilized to create a 'pleasure-dome' for the very people who should have been ruling and guiding and building the galaxy. Well, ruling is a tiresome business, so, after the Isolation Webs had been established around Earth, cutting her off for the Second Separation, no one thought to bother about the rest of the galaxy. Or if they did, they kept it to themselves. Comparing True Humanity with them, indeed!

'What in Floth is he talking about?' asked Undlum, baffled by this reference to brothers and sisters when he knew he was an only child.

'He is talking heresy,' whispered Fovverer, but loud enough to be heard by a few in case it was a clever thing to say.

'No,' said Magrib, being fair for reasons known only to him. (Fovverer coughed and drank some wine.) 'Burgundal is correct. We are closer to them than perhaps we think.'

Burgundal smiled at Magrib and his audience settled once more.

'I have looked out upon mankind. I have discussed with nature herself. I have pondered the future of all. I have discovered that the galaxy is dying of a foul and almost incurable disease.'

Once more he paused for effect, during which time Magrib, repossessing his short-lasted gift of fairness, released a small amount of unwanted gas from his lower intestine which somewhat spoiled the effect of the next word.

'Apathy,' said Burgundal, firmly, his hair still with suppressed rage. He glared at the old, mischevious Human and utilized his mirrors so none other saw that look. However, all the True Humans once more seemed to be with Burgundal.

'That is the illness,' he concluded, a little weakly.

Callastop, reluctant to allow her most-maligned fellow Human such unanimity of support, despite her own apparent concurrence, said dryly, 'And how did you discover that amazing fact?'

Once more Burgundal was unsure of his approach to this. What had started as a mere diversion was now becoming slightly complicated in its effectuation. As most were following his lead with their usual complacency, he could not stop now and surrender to the most annoying Magrib and the obstinate Callastop.

'Well, my good friend Callastop,' he said, in the hope of irritating her sufficiently to quieten her, 'as you surely know, our Ancestors (revere) chose themselves as the optimum humans, the True Humans, and eventually isolated themselves on Earth leaving the remainder of the galaxy to, well, to get on with it alone.

'I have seen the results of mankind's efforts in this direction. Without the pool of genius which our Ancestors represented (my apologies, revere revere) they were as nothing. No progress was made. A genetic decline took place. They live, but without any hope. They have intelligence, but not enough to raise themselves. Or, perhaps, they now have enough, there must be sufficient somewhere, but the apathy has become not merely a symptom, but the actual disease.'

He laid great emphasis on his closing words and was applauded for the speech which may well, as far as he knew, have had a certain truth about it.

'Look,' he said. He raised a finger with the appropriate device upon it cunningly disguised as a knuckle-cap. Before each Human there appeared a moving picture of a workman leaning on his hoe. They could tell it was moving because of the clouds scudding past in the background. The workman's face seemed tired. Not from overwork but some other, indefinable thing. It was not a physical fatigue.

'He does not look so different,' said Fovverer, glancing out from beneath his petal cloak. He was eager to compensate for his earlier gaffe.

No one saw Magrib smile.

Burgundal nodded. 'His family, also, are afflicted with this complaint. See how the fields are badly tended. Look at the ramshackle house. Their apathy must be almost total. Can we stand by and watch mankind, our relations, however distant, die?'

As he said this, the workman, who seemed not quite as thin as the hoe (though this was no surprise as affected narrowness had only recently been a Human fad) fell from his support, and collapsed to the ground. He remained still. Another workman, further away, ignored him, sitting on the weedy earth until he too fell over.

The speeded picture disappeared.

Burgundal could see that the placid deaths of the two men had a sobering effect on the Humans. There seemed to be no possibility other than that they would all be in favour of his plan. He did not touch their minds again, even in the secretive way he had perfected. He saw Magrib smiling, but

Burgundal knew who had won. He felt just a little disturbed at that knowing smile.

He continued: 'What did those men need to make them work; to save their lives and those of their families? They needed something to strive for. Something above money or physical comfort, other than family or fame. They needed a light in the sky to look at and say, "That is what humanity can do. Mankind can outshine the stars. And I am part of mankind. I will do my share." '

Burgundal's voice had risen as he spoke until, finally, he was shouting. Having put aside a portion of his deviousness, he was showing a certain oblique sincerity.

There was a quiet among the True Humans. The wine went untasted for a short time. The wine-birds perched happily on the firefly chandeliers. Tendrils of blue smoke curled from the few resurrected hookahs.

Eventually, Callastop asked, 'You do not, of course, mean a literal light in the sky?'

Burgundal smiled his smile. 'But I do, Callastop.'

After True Humanity agreed to the Great Plan there was much to-ing and fro-ing. Events moved with an urgency long unknown on Earth. And the True Humans, caught (quite often at any rate) in the spirit of the mighty endeavour, worked as one for the first time, perhaps ever. They derived frequent and intense pleasure from their tasks, also, in some perverse way.

In the depths of the planet, those huge machines which had long been employed in retaining such delightful conditions on the surface, now laboured to construct more and different machines, which in turn undertook the activities entrusted to them.

Brainless amoeboid creatures, of frightening enormity but satisfactorily encapsuled, gave freely of their strange secretions, fissioning as never before to produce the maximum in the shortest time. They were soon spent by this but a sufficient quantity of their incandescent fluids had been obtained and stored by then.

Small, thin forces, guided with increasing expertise, sculptured the sub-sub-atomic particles themselves. Mountains (even Magrib's) fell as they were disembowelled for the raw materials within. The sea frothed and steamed while semi-tangible automechs burned goodness from it.

Those were awesome years; rending, fiery, shattering years. The True Humans scarred their mother planet and they felt sure that some of those same scars were cut into them also; but still they toiled on, spending whole hours a month at cushioned computer consoles, expending minute after minute of their invaluable time to ensure that whatever was being done automatically continued to be done automatically.

And they did not labour in vain, for all at once, they were finished.

Burgundal quenched his thirst as a wine-bird fluttered wearily past. He noted that the wine was of poor quality, but what else could be expected after the momentous happenings of late? All would be well after they had built a new home on some suitable world and lived there with justifiable pride and in well-earned solitude.

'We,' he said, after he had once more gathered the right people in the right place which was an easier task than previously, there being only one place remaining, 'have finished. We have changed our home, our Earth,' he noted tears, or their equivalent, in not a few eyes, 'into what will become the brightest, most permanent light in the galaxy. Even far into the centre of the great galactic wheel our burning Earth will be seen and wondered at. We have altered the very structure of matter, robbed ourselves of our birthright, used part of our lives for the sake of mankind. We should feel proud.'

'I offer you an Endless Toast to ourselves.'

'To ourselves,' echoed round with feeling.

Burgundal felt pleased. His diversion had lasted far longer than he had expected and proved reasonably amusing into the bargain. Now it would culminate in something he had not really envisaged when he had begun. A memorial in his own lifetime to himself – and, of course, to True Humanity.

'I have announced to the galaxy my Great Plan. Communications networks have been set up everywhere to broadcast our leaving Earth and firing her. Our vessel, *Mother Earth*, is at the ready. Shall we now depart?'

The True Humans looked about them for one final time. They were all displaying their favourite individual fineries, or whatever decorative accoutrements they felt were suitable. Many sighed at this last view, however changed, of their home planet. It was, except for Burgundal's Tuesday Palace where they and the ship were, a mess of extraordinary tubing; strangely filled holes of impressive depth; untidy mounds; vast elaborate, menacing explosive structures; and seemingly inexplicable, though necessary, constructions of surrealistic appearance. But, though they sighed, this was no time for misgivings, thought Burgundal. Leave those to Magrib who had rarely gone a year without some disparaging remark or another.

He glanced at the withered man who smiled and nodded in response. Burgundal hastened everyone aboard the colossal ship, resplendently adorned with each family's crest and, he now noticed too late, some almost offensive remarks about himself on his own crest. Ignoring this he hurried on, not giving anyone time to become maudlin. He heard Magrib saying that there was no need for a purpose, that True Humanity was no longer capable of great things, then he contrived to shut the old one in a small compartment, accidentally, until the ceremony.

Mother Earth departed, through the Isolation Webs, for a point far outside the solar system. There, with the eyes of the galaxy upon them, the True Humans themselves watched as Burgundal prepared to press the hand-carved button. He had awarded himself this honour.

'For mankind, and all who sail in her,' he said glibly, having thought of the words earlier. His smile, too, contained its little sadness in a well-rehearsed way.

They all looked at the specially dimmed viewers. They smiled with satisfaction, and Burgundal illuminated his forehead sign, as the huge, violent fires started to spread, and the Earth began to glow. They cheered and passed around the only wine-bird they had remembered to bring.

But then they quietened as, on the viewers, they saw the burning stop. Only a few temporary sparks lit up the dead world. Those meagre flashes soon ceased and all that was left was an enormous, charred mass.

The True Humans looked at each other.

They looked at Burgundal.

Their leader in the mighty deed frowned. 'Our Great Plan,' he said generously, 'would appear to have failed. I feel we should not stay,'

Magrib smiled. 'We are not, in fact, so perfect ourselves, Burgundal,' he said.

Burgundal scowled at him.

Mother Earth fled the galaxy just ahead of a wave of laughter, and was hardly ever seen again.

However, the galaxy itself lived on, as did the people in it, long-despised (if thought of at all) by the True Humans though they were.

There was one planet, for instance, where a workman stood leaning on his hoe. The workman was not unlike his father who had died in the same field, but he was of a slightly better build.

Clouds moved slowly in the background. All else was still.

Suddenly, the man sniggered. Then he chuckled, chortled and downright belly-laughed. He looked upwards in the general direction of the lump of ash known as Earth and shook his head, remembering the fiasco called the Great Plan. He began laughing again, and laughed until he had to stop because bits of him hurt.

After that he felt so good he got down to doing some more work.

FACE TO INFINITY

by

E. C. Tubb

Carl possessed everything of prosaic luxury he could desire for his voyage to the stars. As the natural leader with over-riding authority he could enjoy himself in his own way across the light years. Perhaps, had he been a little more ambitious . . .

FACE TO INFINITY

CONSCIOUSNESS rose like a bubble to burst in a rainbow shimmer of expanding awareness; the touch of sheets, the scent of hair, the warmth of a female body close to his own. Other things; the familiar sight of his cabin, the clock with crystal glitters, the wardrobe filled with soft fabrics. And yet more; the low susuration of voices, a murmur barely heard and still less understood.

'It must surely be obvious that for any man to suffer immolation will result in total withdrawal and inevitable insanity.'

'True, but as long as the sensory perceptions are stimulated the ego will look outward, not inward. Insanity is, after all, only a matter of cultural definition.'

Carter and Loomis? He felt a sudden rage, quickly dying. The voices were dull; but the content was familiar. Always they argued on matters of abstruse psychology as if finding intellectual satisfaction in the mouthing of long words. And the voices could belong to no one else – they were far too deep to have belonged to the rest of the crew.

'Honey.' Alice turned, waking, snuggling against him, eyes closed, hands groping like blind kittens, their touch warm and velvet. 'Honey?'

'No.'

'Please!'

'Up,' he said. 'Time to get moving.'

Dressed, he entered the dining hall. Four faces looked at him, two male, two female; all rose and smiled in greeting.

'Good morning, Carl. Have a good night?'

'Sleep well?'

'You look a mite peaked, Carl. Did Alice take it out of you?'

That was Carter, round, suet-pudding of a face wreathed in a smile, pudgy hands lifting as if he were a priest giving benediction. Seated beside him Loomis, his twin, echoed the suggestive snigger. One day, Carl decided, he would do something about the pair. Something peculiarly horrible.

Alice came from behind him and took her place at the table. She was silent as she ate, eyes downcast, knowing it was time for a change and yet hating the thought of losing her favoured position. Yet it would come again, he silently promised, watching the sheen of her long, blonde hair, the curve of her cheek. Gwen, hair as dark as midnight, spooned marmalade on toast and nibbled at the crusty morsel.

'Couldn't we increase the size of the play court?' she asked. 'We could knock down one of the bulkheads and make one big room instead of two smaller ones. I'm dying for a game of tennis.'

'No structural alterations of any kind are permitted,' said Loomis automatically. 'Be content with what you've got.'

'Which is?'

'A damned sight more than anything you were used to before you joined this crew.' Alice was sharp, spiteful, even white teeth flashing like those of a fox. 'If you want to get rid of excess energy how about cleaning the ship?'

'Be quiet, you two!' Cynthia was a red-head and had a temper to match. 'Cleaning is taken in turn. Right, Carl?'

He smiled, enjoying his supremacy, his position of power. Girls, he thought, they always like to be close to the one in authority. But he had to play fair.

'That's right,' he agreed. 'Alice cleans the ship. Loomis?'

'Check all systems.'

'Monitor the sensors,' said Carter.

Cynthia hesitated. 'Void all waste matter.'

'Tally the stores,' said Gwen.

'Then do it,' said Carl.

It was routine; a matter of moving from one part of the ship to another, checking, testing, seeing that everything was as it should be and that nothing had gone wrong. But nothing could go wrong – the concept was unthinkable.

Back in the recreation room they settled to take care of the rest of the day. Carter and Gwen played chess, the others made up a four at bridge. The cards were shining-clean, crisp to the fingers, the surfaces unworn.

The sound of their bids echoed like the chime of bells.

'One club,' said Loomis.

'Two diamonds,' said Alice.

'Three clubs,' said Cynthia.

'Four no trumps,' said Carl.

He won, he always won, the others by now owed him a sum greater than the national debt. One day, perhaps, he would collect.

Bored he rose and went forward to where the great screens showed the eternal vista of the stars. For a long time he studied them, wondering how far they had come, how much further they would have to go. Years? Decades? It was possible; but what of it? They were comfortable in their haven. The showers always ran hot and cold, the food was delicious, the company mostly pleasant and, when it wasn't, he could quickly bring it back into line.

He turned at a faint noise. Cynthia was standing just behind him, the expression in her eyes unmistakable.

'Carl,' she murmured. 'When is it going to be my turn again? Loomis is—' Her arms circled his body and dragged him close to her warm contours. 'Carl?'

He struggled against her arms. They clutched even tighter.

'Carl!' Her voice had deepened, grown thick and demanding. The white gleam of fangs showed behind the full redness of her lips. They touched his throat, nipped, began to penetrate the skin. 'I need you, Carl. I need you!'

He twisted, feeling pain at his throat, thrusting the woman from him with a jerk of his arms. For a moment the control room wheeled in a circle of brilliant glitters then it steadied and was as before.

'Carl?' The woman looked at him and was just that – a woman pleading to be loved.

'Later,' he said, and walked from the place of star-bright screens and watchful dials.

He heard the murmur as he entered the recreation room. Carter and Loomis, heads together, muttering their endless litany of esoteric knowledge. They parted as he approached.

'Carl?'

'Alice,' he snapped. 'I want her. Where is she?'

Carter blinked. 'Alice?'

'Yes, Alice, you fool!'

Loomis cleared his throat. 'Carl, who is Alice?'

One day, thought Carl, I will kill him. I will take him and spread him out, split him down the middle and open his guts to the sky. The sky and the waiting vultures. Him and Carter both. I will get the pair of them all in my own good time.

'Alice,' said Loomis. 'Of course. Let's go and find her.'

She wasn't to be found.

Somehow she had vanished from the ship – but how? The tell-tales showed that no port had been opened and, anyway, they couldn't be opened from anywhere but the control room and then only after long and tedious formalities. But she wasn't in the recreation room, the dining room, the swimming pool, the showers, the kitchens, the theatre, the shooting range, the play room, the library, the laboratory, the conservatory, the observatory. She wasn't in the bedrooms, the dark room, the music room. Nor on the promenade. She had simply vanished.

Or had been made to vanish.

Carl thought about it as, the others at his heels, he strode through the echoing vastness of the ship. One or more of the others must have killed her and disposed of her body. But that too was impossible. A human body held a lot of meat, a lot of blood and bone. To pass it through the voider would take time and leave stains. There had been no time and there were no stains. Yet she could not be found.

Back in the recreation room Cynthia said, 'Could something have come aboard? An invisible something from out there?' The movement of her hand signalled the great emptiness beyond the hull.

'Impossible!' Carter was firm. 'If such a thing was intangible enough to pass through metal then it would have been too insubstantial to snare a human being. And, even if something could have managed to enter the ship, how could it have taken Alice out?'

'It could have dematerialized her,' said Gwen. 'It could have extended the matter of her material being until it had achieved a permeable tenuosity.'

'That means we must have breathed in a part of her body,' said Loomis. He was thoughtful. 'In a sense we have incorporated her into ourselves.'

'A closed, feed-back cycle,' agreed Carter. 'She is us and we are her. That means we must all share her appetite. Shall we eat?'

'No,' said Carl.

He was, naturally, obeyed.

That evening Cynthia died.

It was evening only by convention, there was no real time aboard the vessel, but the habit of regular hours was a psychological necessity in order to maintain the workings of the biological clock. Carl heard the scream, the thick slobbering giggle, saw the horror as he burst into the kitchen.

Gwen stood over a moaning figure, a knife in her hand. As she saw him she stooped and plunged it into Cynthia's body. A fountain of blood spurted from the ripped abdomen, staining her dress, painting her face into a devil's mask. Giggling she threw aside the knife and draped her neck with smoking entrails. Kneeling she thrust her face into the puddle of blood oozing from the gaping wound.

'My God!' Carter turned away, retching. 'No! No, I didn't mean – for God's sake do something!'

'It has all been taken care of.' Loomis, with his bland, hateful face, his too-ready smile. 'The trauma will not last and soon the conviction that all is normal will overwhelm the sense of disorientation. There is no need for concern.'

Carl knocked him aside, slamming the kitchen door and locking it as he cut off the sight of the horror within. Sweating he stood against the panel, heard the thud from the other side, doubled as pain lanced his side to blur his vision with spinning darkness. Dimly he heard the thick, inhuman voice, snarling an impotent rage.

'I'll get you! I'll get you if it's the last thing I do! You won't get away with this, damn you! You sadistic perverts! You monsters! You filthy, degenerate swine! I'll make you pay for what you've done to me!'

His voice, and then another, cool, hatefully calm.

'Steady now, Carl. Just relax and take it easy.'

Carter stood before him, smiling, something bright and shining in his hand. He lifted it, aimed, thrust it directly into Carl's neck. Pain from the lacerated throat merged with the dull agony in his side. He tried to run and fell to lie sprawled on the floor looking up at the two men.

'An expected reaction,' said Loomis with chill detachment.

'Beneficial?'

'Unfortunately, no, but it will pass. Everything will pass. A hundred years from now and all will be forgotten.'

'Damn you!' Carl climbed painfully to his feet. His legs felt numb, dead, appendages without feeling or function. He blinked to clear his eyes of crystal glitters, feeling a new terror. 'The ship!' he gasped. 'Something is wrong with the ship!'

Loomis smiled, his head shrinking, to grow round and studded with eyes. His body dropped, sprouted legs, grew a thick, ugly covering tufted with sparse fur. On multiple legs the spider scuttled up the wall to hang watching with glittering eyes.

'Carter!' He turned to the other man. 'Help me, damn you. Help me!'

'To do what, Carl?'

'To get out of here, man. What else? To get out of here!'

Solemnly Carter shook his head.

'I'm afraid that is quite impossible, Carl. After all you did volunteer, and surely this is better than spending your life in a cell? Five years, perhaps less, and you will be free. Just five, short years. And you will not suffer, I promise you that.'

'You bastard! I didn't know. I didn't guess! For God's sake get me out of here!'

He ran from the empty smile, racing through endless corridors, endless rooms, running until the breath rasped in his lungs and his muscles trembled with exhaustion. Finally he halted to stare at a black loathsome body, a smiling mask which gently swayed from side to side.

'I told you,' said Carter. 'It is quite impossible to escape. Now why not be sensible and make the best of things? The connections are all made and cannot be unmade. And think of the adventure!'

'You said five years?'

'Maybe a little more; but it will be your time, Carl, not ours. We shall all be dead by then. But you will be expected

136

and science will have progressed far enough then to do what we cannot. So have hope, my friend. Hope . . . hope . . . hope . . .'

Hope!

The name of the ship.

The only thing left to him.

The only promise to be found in a universe of pain and terror, the machinations of science and the bleakness of despair.

To hope and to continue hoping for now and forever.

But first must come revenge.

He flung himself at the smiling face, hands reaching to rip and tear, to maim and to kill. Beneath his hands Carter moaned and then began to melt, to fall and end in a thin, oozing mat of slime on the floor. From the slime lifted a hundred grasping hands, a thousand sprouting eyes, ten thousand gaping mouths all gusting an acrid vapour.

Blinded, terrified, he ran from the scene, slammed into a bulkhead, turned and again met the stunning impact of un-yielding metal. When next he threw himself forward he felt the bite of strands about his limbs, the constricting material of a web holding him close, closer, binding him tight until he could hardly breathe and found it impossible to move.

On the wall the spider moved, swinging from side to side, spinning, becoming a blurred circle of eye-bright glitters which grew and grew until there was nothing in the universe but the overwhelming, hypnotic shimmer.

Carl groaned and looked at the thing just above his face, at the wheeling points of light, bright and clean in their random motion. He could see, in the reflection of the stain-less steel eighteen inches above, the lined and ravaged face, the complex helmet with the trailing wires, the pipes buried in his arms and throat, the thick cables sprouting from the support cradling his head.

The cables wired into the 'dead' areas of his brain, the nine tenths for which the only use was to function now as the living computer of the ship. His ship. The *Hope* of which he was the guiding part.

The probe sent out to circle a distant star and to return to Earth – one day.

Rolling his eyes he could see, just to one side, the cause of the breakdown. Drifting globules had already sealed the tiny hole but the damage had been done. A tiny meteor had penetrated the hull and smashed the dream-mechanism on which his sanity depended.

Now there would be no more dreams, no women, no company, no illusion of space and gracious living.

There would be nothing but the endless years in which, locked in a metal coffin, he would go inevitably and totally insane.

But he wouldn't die. The machines would see to that.

THE CALL OF THE WILD

by

Manuel van Loggem

With a few elegantly deceptive gestures Manuel van Loggem draws us into the heart of this nightmare situation of a future that is quite impossible. Perhaps it is only an apparent impossibility; perhaps the Federation is already surreptitiously at work, propagandizing, recruiting, awaiting the day their recreation becomes legal. The newspapers carry accounts of their sporting activities every day ... Maybe we all need to use a petrol atomizer to freshen up.

THE CALL OF THE WILD

THE NEW recreation originated in Paris, but by now clubs have already sprung up in most of the capitals of Europe. They have joined the international federation which has laid down the rules of the game. Already there are plans to organize world championships. Of course Paris will be the first city to have the honor of receiving the crack performers, but there still remain some legal objections. Foreigners taking part in the games ought to have the same rights and duties as residents. Some exploratory trials have been held, but they have not yet produced a clear verdict. A foreigner who wishes to pursue his sport in Paris still runs the risk of being seized as an ordinary criminal. Furthermore, France lays down the death penalty for premeditated murder.

One can understand how these old-fashioned regulations greatly hinder the desire to participate. They also hamper the healthy development of the hunting. For nothing is as good for a new sport as international matches, which help to improve the quality of the performances, at the same time providing excellent propaganda for those who are still outsiders. But in Paris itself the season for pedestrians has just been declared open. The first Tuesday in Autumn has been set aside for it. At that time there are always many strangers in the City of Light. Most of them don't know the rules of the game very well and can be easily caught. Voices have been raised in favor of keeping people who are ignorant of the rules from becoming victims; but for practical reasons this could not be realized, for it would imply providing these people with a recognizable sign, and that would mean that they would be informed of the rules, and consequently the sign in question would be useless.

The decision was that all pedestrians, including the ignorant, may be hunted. Of course there is less honor to be won than with able dodgers; but for many hunters it is no great matter. Any sport has its participants who care more for visible bounty than for inner satisfaction.

'Better one body on the bumper than ten points on the list of honor' is their slogan, and one cannot do very much against it as long as they keep themselves within the boundaries of the rules.

I had a conversation about these problems with the Chairman of the Board of the Union of Pedestrian Hunters, M. Pierre Chasseur, who has his office in the Rue de la Paix. He received me with remarkable kindness; but, also, somehow condescendingly.

'They are still fishing in your country?' he asked with the exaggerated tone of sauvity one often finds in high officials.

'Yes,' I confessed. 'With us there is still a lot of fishing.'

'Not any more, here,' he said, with satisfaction. 'At least, not in our circles. Hunting pedestrians has entirely replaced angling here. It's a much more fascinating sport.'

He told me, not without pride, of his efforts to get the new sport legalized.

'It has cost me much time and trouble, but now we have the full cooperation of the authorities. Many diplomats are already members of our club. As you might know, the pedestrian has been hunted a great deal before this time, but it was all too wild, too irregular, and too unsporting. That's different now.'

He rose and paced enthusiastically to and fro. He was much smaller than I had estimated. He twirled his thin yellow moustache until he had made two sharp points of it. Once in a while he sprayed himself with petrol from a small perfume bottle.

Then we discussed possibilities of distributing propaganda for the new sport in my country. I told him of the severe objections that still existed there. Pedestrian hunting is still considered a bizarre and particularly shocking game by my countrymen.

'What nonsense!' was M. Chasseur's opinion. 'In the beginning it was the same here. But people soon get used to it, as they do to bullfights. Once that is accomplished, one is able to appreciate the beauty of the sport, the skill, insight, and intelligence necessary to land a pedestrian according to the rules. The rules in themselves are intricate enough. Last week we passed an amendment to the effect that extra points can be awarded for Americans. They are such well-trained road-jumpers that it's hard to get them on your bumper. For that matter, the pedestrian is not defenceless. When he sticks to the rules, it's tough work to get him. At this time it's far more difficult to bag a decent bounty than at the beginning. The pedestrians have become much more careful. You know they are safe on the zebras, and now there are many who already instinctively avoid the prohibited paths. A great number have begun to wait for stop lights, and there are even some who confine themselves strictly to the traffic laws. So you need to use intelligence for a good hunt. You may have noticed it yourself.'

I nodded. It was a fact that one saw fewer cars with pedestrians tied to the fender than at the start of the hunting season last year.

'I've been told that some hunters have used inadmissable methods,' I remarked, hesitating slightly, for fear of insulting my host. But he took it in a sporting fashion.

'It's true,' he said. 'Especially with the new members, it has occurred from time to time. From the lower circles. But we take strong measures against it. They are expelled as soon as we have sufficient proof. That means the revoking of their hunting licence. I know that some hunters have let a well-constructed young girl walk alluringly in front of their cars, or have tossed coins outside the zebra stripes. But that doesn't help any more. The pedestrians are smarter than you think. They soon caught on.'

'In any case, in our country the sport is considered rather cruel,' I said. 'In Parliament, even, questions have been raised concerning it. The Society of Pedestrians is asking for prohibition of the hunting, at any rate for members of the organization who wear the membership badge.'

M. Chasseur started. He splashed himself again with petrol, and sat down once more behind his Empire writing desk.

'I didn't know that,' he murmured. 'I think that's awfully unsporting of them, and unfair, too. You know that we as hunters especially want to promote the preservation of the pedestrian. We only hunt those who violate the traffic regulations. You surely must know that in the first few months after the opening of the season the number of people killed on the roads diminished by thirty percent, and that is because the pedestrians have grown much more cautious. They are no longer as defenceless as they used to be when everybody could hunt them as they pleased. Pedestrians who are well-acquainted with the rules have a much better chance of survival than they used to have. That's to our advantage, too, for this way the stock of pedestrians remains up to the mark. Under eighteen and over sixty they may not be hunted, either, even if they are standing in the middle of the freeway.'

'But how can you tell their age from your car?' I asked.

'The Union Nationale des Piétons distributes age-bands to their members, but now pedestrians have appeared on the streets with counterfeit bands, and that has nothing to do with sport any more.'

He again twirled his moustache, but in the reverse direction, so that it looked like a length of frayed rope. He looked at his watch.

'In a few minutes I have an appointment with a man from Sweden,' he said. 'In the café on the other side of the street. I would appreciate it if you could come with me for a small drink. Then we could talk about founding a branch of the Federation in your country.'

He went out before me. With obvious delight he sniffed the blue clouds of exhaust fumes hanging in the street.

'Good weather for hunting,' he said.

When we were in the middle of the street, a gleaming asphalt frigate suddenly came screaming around the corner and headed straight for us.

With two heart-wrenchingly startled jumps, I was able to make it safely to the pavement.

I saw a young man step out of the car and with practiced movements strap M. Chasseur to the fender.

And then I perceived from the small flecks of blood on the street that my companion had in his enthusiasm for one moment overstepped the boundaries of the zebra.

WORDSMITH

by

BRYN FORTEY

*It is not easy to be a writer. It is also not easy to under-
stand just what that statement means, unless you have par-
ticipated in some of the agony yourself. Bryn Fortey's story
introduces, among other delicacies, the extravagant and in-
toxicating notion of Black Art, the Stealer of Dreams. If,
among the plethora of problems a writer faces, he must now
take into consideration the problem of his own versions of
Black Art, the agony must inevitably increase exponen-
tially. No wonder that Piller Presavorrat, wordsmith, decided to wear no face.*

WORDSMITH

NOBODY *wrote*. Not anymore. A subject, rendered unconscious and with induced mental irritation, was crowned with a net of micronic impulse absorbers. Deep-down, root-level brain activity was picked up, driven along plastic coated wires and punched onto coded reels of tape. These were automatically transcribed into sheets of typewritten words.

That's the modern publishing game.

That's why only insane subjects provide best sellers.

Piller Presavorrat knew this but dodged all obvious conclusions with complete determination. He produced words, all dragged with blood and sweat from his own mind – through his own effort. Piller was a writer, and that was the end of the news.

Piller Presavorrat: Writer (unpublished).

He submitted manuscripts, pestered publishers, wrote bitchy letters to the press, and achieved nothing but sweet zero. Most publishers hated him and very few would even read his submissions before rejecting. He was a throwback, fifty years out of date and seemingly unaware of modern trends.

The dinosaur is best extinct.

It hurt, this constant failure, of course it did. All that creativity down the pan and flushed away with only a gurgle in the pipework to show it had ever existed at all. But wasn't that the way of things, and hadn't it always been, in spite of early hope and ambition?

The party had been a wasted effort as far as furthering his nonexistent career was concerned; but the free booze had been one consolation, and a surplus of available women had been another. Especially one who had found this strange wordsmith an attractive proposition.

'I write of love and hate,' Piller had told her. His hand

cupped her breast, thumb flicking the nipple. 'I paint word pictures of stark truth and beauty. The printed page is my canvas.' He had blown into her ear, nipping the lobe between his teeth and nuzzling gently against her hair. 'One day my talent will reinstate the creative art of the written word.'

'I'm sure it will,' she had agreed, not understanding a single word, but fascinated by his fanaticism.

Presavorrat yearned to write in an age when the art had become redundant. No publisher was without a highly paid consultant psychiatrist, and readers wanted only to bask in the deep dredged thought processes of the mad.

Slopping drink over himself and the floor, Piller had staggered across to where a high priest had held court. 'Art is dead!' he'd cried, nailed to the cross of his own futility. 'You have killed it, and are killing me.'

The publisher had raised a nonchalant eyebrow.

'You are dirty, homosexual, philistine bums. No, I retract that. Some of you are, or might be, but not all. I mustn't generalize, but you do all sacrifice your everything upon the altar of fame and gain. Surely you could take one single chance for the sake of genuine human endeavour!'

Bored, the publisher had turned away.

Heavy time tonight, thought the girl who intended going home with him. Piller seemed the sort who got randy when drunk.

And she had been right!

'I will be published one day,' he muttered between grunts.

'No, Piller, please. Don't talk about writing when we're making love!'

He had wanted to tell her about how he hated all publishers, but he held back. She was right, of course, and he knew it.

Real love and genuine hate, opposite ends of the same spectrum, were areas that deserved total dedication. Neither warranted mindless intrusion, and were too close for one to overlap into the other. His love for her should be kept separate from all other considerations. Free from the frustrations of his life style. Untouched by all other relationships. A pocket of safety. A sanctuary from a world that misunderstood and misused him.

148

'I love only you!' he said, harshly, their sweat drenched bodies slipping and sliding in a riot of movement. And I hate all the others, he thought with a stark simplicity that turned his act of love into a moment of mere lust, and left him feeling dirty about it all.

In that instant he knew sin and blanked his mind with a death rattle whisper like the tearing of ancient silk. His head seemed to explode, gushing globulets of brain all along a gutter.

Why is it that childhood hopes have to grow into adult reality? he wondered; but sleep claimed before an answer could even be considered. A sleep that brought no peace, only scenes that jumped and jerked before bloodshot eyes as the wordsmith grovelled in his own excreta. An idea lay dead, crushed by thoughts wrenched hard from lunatic fantasies.

Blank, loveless eyes proclaim yet another victim of the self destructive process. There is something here that causes fear.

Presavorrat stood upon a dusty plain. Beyond him a mountain grew up to the sky. Somewhere, up high, a wise man waited, but the terrain was too difficult for him to master.

Presavorrat wept, his hot tears irrigating the arid landscape. He stood in an area of disembodied failure, denying the sense of belonging that tried to fit so snugly around his drooping shoulders.

'The system *can* be broken,' he grated through clenched teeth, and a flower emerged from the tear stained sand.

The treadmills keep turning, but Piller still dreams of the day when written words will once again replace extracted thoughts.

Presavorrat awoke, retinas hurting in the pale morning light. Her arm lay across his bare chest.

Today I will start a new novel, he decided, and this woman will be my inspiration.

'Jay Morast,' he murmured aloud, bringing to mind the twelve month old affair of the man with no face. Yesterday's headlines now, but what a story could be made of the case.

The old excitement ran through him.

It was a gallop that cleansed. A glorious jaunt across fields of heather to a land of sparkling waterfalls. Hope was the means of transport and belief the power that drove.

Golden highways popped in his mindseye.

The woman having been versed in the silent, non-stop supply of coffee, Piller prepared himself for a new onslaught on greatness. A pile of blank white sheets lay to the right of his machine. A virgin space to the left awaited the filled pages.

Presavorrat inserted a blank sheet. '*THE MAN WITH NO FACE*', he typed, '*by Piller Presavorrat*'. Fingers poised above the keyboard, he concentrated his total self towards the act of creation upon which he was about to embark. At the appointed moment, his fingers flashed downwards. He was writing. A wordsmith, concocting letters to his own patterns and designs. An archaic pastime, but one that nevertheless provided the only substance that could keep the threads of his life from fraying completely.

Presavorrat typed on.

'*"No right to survive such an operation."*

"He had no business surviving an explosion like that in the first place."

"It's always a miracle when someone lives through an accident in space."

"Accident? I wonder."

Nearing the surface at fleeting moments, the patient in the private ward picked up vaguely heard phrases and blurred impressions before lapsing back into the state of complete unknowing the hospital tried to keep him in.

"It might have been kinder if we'd let him die!"

Jay Morast was a man without a face. Instead of it the surgeons had provided a blank frame upon which he could fit features, as in a jigsaw.

"Not many people who can genuinely change their face to fit their moods," joked the pretty little night nurse.

Morast selected a look of love, and welcomed her into his bed.

What a sucker he had been: universal fall guy, number one. Smuggling, they'd told him. Looks a clapped out wreck; but that is just a cover to fool the law. Goes like a bomb really. Sure enough, it did too. Blew up just like a bomb.

Out there in space, half-way between Earth and Mars. An ask-no-questions, out-of-work, spaceline pilot conned into a nonexistent smuggling job which turned out to be an insurance caper.

And the bastards had meant him to die!

It was this thought alone that made him welcome his survival during the long, long months of recuperation that followed the surgery. Jay Morast was a man without a face, and someone was going to have to pay for it.

"It's like being made love to by a different man every night," said the pretty little night nurse. "As you change your face, so your performance varies to match the newly selected features."

She hoped his recuperation would last for years.

"What can I expect tonight?" she asked, then screamed as he revealed his face of death.

The doctors were worried in case seeing someone die from a heart attack might affect his recovery. The new night nurse was worried in case she might share her predecessor's misfortune.

Both sets of fears were soon calmed. Much to the doctors' surprise, he showed an even keener rate of improvement than before. As for the new nurse, well, her concern soon disappeared along with her inhibitions and uniform. In Morast's bed, seemingly in the arms of a different man each night, she came alive for the first time in her life. A short life that stretched from death to death. From the heart attack of the previous nurse until the time when she herself leapt from the window of the tenth floor private ward. Before anyone could reach his room, Jay Morast had replaced his look of terror with one of repose.

He was ready now, and knew it. Ready to revenge himself upon those who had sent him into space to die. Not even Black Art, who came in dreams and sneeringly offered his face to replace the one Morast had left in space, could spoil the gleeful anticipation of his vendetta.

Black Art, an intended character in a novel left unwritten. Denied even the fictional reality of his original conception, he roamed the dark alleys of night. A stealer of dreams, with abuse and hate his only weapons.

"Where's your face then, Morast? We both know it, a facial cripple is all, man. You dig? A facial cripple.

"I should have organized the bang that got you. Dead then, and better off for being so.

"Want to borrow a face, Morast? My face? A big, black face? A big black real face? I'd rather wander dreams than have your blank frame and false features." '

Presavorrat stopped typing, fingers twitching to a halt as his mind caught up with what he had written. It had all been flowing so well, as planned, until the unbidden appearance of Black Art.

What the hell had made him bring in that character?

Getting up from his stool, Presavorrat paced the room. It had been years since he had invented Black Art, a Negro private eye who smashed crime syndicates throughout the whole system. It was, he remembered, after the National Film Library had run a series of illustrated lectures on the social significance of the bygone Shaft films. He had shelved the idea before typing even one word, realizing that he was doing no more than update the old Shaft character. And he hadn't brought Black Art to mind from that day to this.

It was strange, and yet the idea had merit. An unwritten character whose only recourse was to invade dreams in a forlorn search for the reality forever denied him. A pseudo-being, held fast by the suction of night.

An excitement shook him to the very root of his ego. This could be his breakthrough. This could be the concept with which he could rival the extracted gibberings of the insane. This would be the novel to herald back the redundant art of the wordsmith!

The woman entered then, with coffee that was soon forgotten as Presavorrat danced her around the room. He babbled words which left her bemused, but his joy was infectious and she was happy because he was. She understood little of the motivating factors that drove him so remorselessly, but knew well the personal contribution that was demanded of her.

'Dream trips go no way towards providing true form and reality,' said Presavorrat as he broke into a tango that headed straight for the bedroom door.

'I believe you, Piller,' she replied with a laugh. Life with a wordsmith was anything but dull.

Later, as train whistles screeched, screamed, and all tracks led to a tunnel in the rock-face, Presavorrat slept. A restless slumber of twisted sheets and lumpy pillows, full of dark alley whimpers and whispered obscenities.

'Poor Piller,' murmured the woman as he tossed and turned, little realizing that out of the formless night patterns Black Art was making his dream presence felt.

Big and strong, dark as the night that claimed him, Black Art came to Presavorrat while he slept. 'Look at me, man,' he ordered. 'Powerful, cruel, a winner all the way. A creation destined for fictional greatness, but you shelved the idea and booked me passage on the oblivion express. Hell, baby, I would have had it made!'

Sleeping, Presavorrat suffered the blast of raw power until it seemed he would drown in his own mattress. Art towered over him, ferocious in his anger. 'I would have been great!' he thundered.

'But publishers don't want written words,' Presavorrat managed to whisper through his fear. 'They'll accept nothing but extracted thoughts.'

'If you were good enough you'd make it. Just a hack. No talent, no courage, no nothing. You'll never break the stranglehold of the extracters, not without a character like me to make life leap and tingle through your pages.'

Denied even the fictional reality of his original conception, Black Art loomed malignantly over his dream trapped creator. 'Write me, you bastard!' he demanded. 'Give me that much or by all that's unholy I swear to sever the chains that bind me and enfold your existence to replace the one you dangled so tantalisingly then withdrew.'

Presavorrat could only scream as big black hands reached out towards him. Red tinged screams that seemed to pour from a gash, a second mouth in the throat of humanity.

Black blood spurted like demented rain, producing a rich cancer that would melt in daylight. Green sparks fusing brains that plunged towards the pit.

Presavorrat wept and the hands that reached out made fists that shook with threatened violence. 'You owe me!'

shrieked Black Art with impotent rage as he faded into nocturnal mists.

The woman held him tightly, cradling him to her breast. 'There, there,' she cooed gently, 'everything will be all right.' But two hours later Piller still wept and muttered. 'Black as the abyss,' he said between tears. 'After my life.'

The woman could make no sense from any of it. Not from his non-stop crying nor his insane ramblings. 'Hell spawned, from the depths of my mind,' he muttered as he sobbed. The realization finally came home to her that she was powerless in every way.

The doctor she sent for decided he was also unable to help, apart for arranging for hospitalization and expert opinion.

Poor Piller, thought the woman, closing the door on yet another episode. Insane, they said. Completely, utterly, and with little hope of a cure. For her he was now relegated to the past, but for others he was very much the present.

The psychiatrist in charge of his case telephoned the publisher who paid him an annual retainer. 'Got a sure-fire smash for you this time,' he claimed with supreme confidence. 'A real dilly, as you will agree after reading the case notes I'm sending.'

The publisher did agree, and wasted no time setting up a thought extraction session. This one really did have best selling potential.

It wasn't the way he had planned, and he no longer knew anything about it, but his life-long ambition was soon to be realized. Piller Presavorrat, wordsmith, was heading for publication.

MANGANON

by

Michael Stall

Michael Stall's vision here, incorporating the farthest reaches of the future and the farthest reaches of the past that turn out to be the day before yesterday, contains an evocative creation of the true otherness of a world that, for all Gwent knew at first, could be fact or fantasy, hell or purgatory. For George Gwent and for Hrunting, two men who came to Manganon from greatly dissimilar backgrounds, the axon gateways offered vastly different prospects, aims that they had not so far revealed. There was much more to Manganon than appeared after the enigma had been solved. Manganon, with its facetted sky, its ceramic weapons, its living armour, its vegetables artifacts and the bewildered people of another time, would, as Michael Stall effortlessly points out, be argued over in the very finest academic style by the bedazzled observers. But, then, the true Manganon was none of these things.

MANGANON

Part One: The Borrowed Sword

I

There was dew on the heather. It was beginning to penetrate the leather bindings on his legs. The Traveller who was currently known as Passer by Gates noted it, and quickly suppressed an associated memory chain. The name he now carried was also beginning to accumulate too many memories, and it had not even been of his own choosing: the other names he had held dredged themselves up: Hraegl, the Aetheling, Siwardsson ... It was a long list, and he took no particular pride in it. But now, in the fruitless search for anonymity, it needed adding to, and the choice was easy: the old words were the best for such things: Hrunting, the borrowed sword.

He looked up: the deep green tracery of the night sky was yielding to the magenta of day. The care *they* took of their charges, even down to maintaining the circadian rhythms! He looked about, over the plain that yielded in the direction – meaninglessly called the East – to minor mountains, beyond them the sea, and down from their maritime watershed a fair river running its once for all way with villages and hamlets dotted about its bottom lands, and a great city at the merging of the waters. Neither city nor village nor sea interested Hrunting: only the Gate that was there, somewhere, perhaps the great dream of all Travellers: an unlooped Axon Gate!

He looked down at the now sodden leathers on his legs, and they brought to mind a sudden rain in the Morea – in primary time – and his Varangians cutting Hauteville hirelings from their horses, and for a moment his fingers half-felt the form of an axe's haft, before the certain futility of it all recalled itself to him.

He felt a dozen aches: this body had scarcely a good year left in it, but that was only to be expected: he had been walking it now three days with scant rest, and that was the pattern of the past year. He could not wait too long before the next Gate, though his eagerness was augmented by the rumour that this coming Gate had a Magister Portarum.

Without thought of rest, the newly renamed Hrunting trudged forward in an empty direction, laved of hope and beyond despair.

2

The road was leading nowhere, only deeper into the Dale Country, away from the warren of cities where Gwent could mantle himself in the nondescript generality – or could have done. There was no pain now, but slowly, almost pleasantly blood oozed through the wad of handkerchiefs out on to the red plastic of the seat. He was dying. He felt little fear: his stomach was too badly torn up by police bullets to tighten, and the numbness that encircled the wound seemed somehow to have spread to his mind. Wearily, he eased off the accelerator and let the car coast to a halt, methodically turning off the ignition and easing on the hand brake. It was not his car: the very least he could do would be to leave it in good condition for its unknown owner: the blood, after all, would wash off, a flake from the snake-skin of reality, like the nine days' wonder of its being stolen by George Gwent, the famed terrorist.

Tiredly, he leaned to take one of the leaflets from the back seat: the bold, cheaply printed 'Free England' banner in red over the black, blood and soil text, stared at him, and had no meaning for him. That was someone else's struggle now. He crumpled it, and wiped ineffectually at the stain on the seat. Then it crossed his mind that if he died in the car, the EPC Auxiliaries might suspect a booby trap and plant a charge. The French Auxiliaries were notably wary, and it was a fifty-fifty chance that they, and not the regular police, would find him first. In his dull, bemused state, the sense of obligation to the car's unknown owner assumed huge proportions. He dropped the dirtied leaflet, and holding the wad in place over the wound, he fumbled the door open and staggered out.

He could see the stars, haloed in his unfocussed vision, and he felt the silence of the night like a blanket held over him, a blanket that magnified the erratic beat of his heart as it relentlessly evacuated the lifeblood in him, turning his trousers into hardening cylinders that impeded knee movement. With his free hand, he delved into his jacket pocket, grasping the ancient Webley. He managed a few paces, out of the zone of brightness he had made opening the car door, before he fell, not in classic movie slow motion but hard on to earth and stone.

He lay motionless for a while, minutes perhaps; it was hard to tell, but finally he noticed the inscribed slab. It had been discarded at the roadside was his first thought – an old gravestone. Appropriate. There was a time of scant consciousness again, then a dull wakefulness. In the low power light of the car interior roof light, yards away, he could make out a few words, in terrible dog latin, old and roughly carved.

'Ego . . . Petrus de Wyke, Magister Porte . . .'

The words held him: 'Magister Porte,' Master of the Gate. It was no title he had ever seen before, and he had read old charters and statutes for years, dredging up pointless precedents and laws for the Movement, in the days before all sides had ceased to respect anything but the gun. Armiger, barone, miles . . . they meant something, but . . . He was confused, tired; he tried to make out more, but everything blurred, faded into the blackness that disguised hedgerow and distant tree, save for one phrase that penetrated the fog that was settling about his mind: '. . . hac porta . . .' By this gate. What gate, and what by it? He turned laboriously over, so that he could see the stars, but his eyes could make out nothing now but utter, unrelieved blackness, like the blackness before the beginning of things. He wrenched the Webley from his pocket, releasing hold of the soaked wad that pent his guts, and held the pistol in a marksman's double grip, determined to break this blackness by gun blazes of creation, but the hammer clicked on an empty chamber.

'... hac porta ...' By this gate. His mind was wandering. Was this death, this primeval numbness that was spreading even to the extremities of his limbs? For a moment, he knew anger.

'I am!' he screamed, or imagined he screamed, and then the numbing blackness seeped finally into his mind, became a torrent, and the universe died, uncreated.

3

There was no transition. For the vision blur of the night sky, a canopy of glowing magenta substituted itself. Gwent stood stock still, observing no fear reactions in himself; this was too strange quickly to excite fear. As he thought about it, then his heart would begin to pound, his ...

Stood! He was standing! He hurt no more! A glance revealed his clothes still tattered, but clean, with no wounds beneath them. He had been dying, and he was alive, here! He looked hard at the new sky: there was more difference here than colour: he could make out a faint tracery of lines, as if the sky itself were faceted, and he himself stood in the very centre of an enormous jewel.

Palpably, he did not. All around him, scarcely looking odd even in the reddish light, were the normal accoutrements of the moor, grass, bushes, the occasional tree. It was that normality amidst strangeness that finally set his heart pounding.

How long he stood there, silent, unmoving, he didn't know. Fear mounted in waves, beat a surf of terror over him, then scattered in froth to reveal yet more and larger waves ... With as great an effort of will as he had ever made, he broke the pattern. Whatever had happened had to have a rational explanation, not necessarily a pleasant one, but a rational one. With such thoughts he slowed the trip hammer in his chest, slowing it to a heartbeat.

Am I dreaming? he thought suddenly, but the answer supplied itself: every dream he could recall always had a saving air of unreality that either frustratingly shadowed its joys or thankfully diminished its horrors – an element of conscious reality intruding. Here, sense, feeling, intuition all shouted at him: this is for real!

An alternate world? Another planet? But the facetted sky! Insanity seemed the best bet; but didn't the insane never even consider that possibility, or was that just folk-lore? It didn't matter; he wasn't seriously considering it as a possibility. The truth was he had insufficient data for a useful judgment, so – gather more. He walked.

And as he walked, normalcy enveloped him, words formed themselves in sequential order in his mind – sequential, for causality seemed still to be valid here. He tried to think about it; but his thoughts merely fitted themselves to the old grooves. He noticed a clump of bushes surmounted by a tree, a miniature copse. He sat down on the grass, his back to the copse and wondered what time of day it was. As there was no sun—

The breath came out of him in a single, lung emptying gasp. He'd realized it before, but even in his mind he'd been afraid to verbalize it. Now it was out. He had not stumbled by accident on some bizarre warp or fissure in space-time: his new environment was artificial. This was not elsewhere . . . it was a made thing. He—

There was a rustling behind him. He came to his feet, twisting about to see a short, wild figure, all beard and eyes, in a leather jack and russets thonged to mid calf, and all topped by a battered but still serviceable plain helmet. Gwent did not fail to notice the scramasax the newcomer clutched in his right hand.

'What do you want?' he rapped out, without thinking whether the newcomer could understand English.

The warrior twisted his face under the beard: 'I'm going to carve you a little, brother.'

'Why?' Gwent replied, with a dispassionate calm that surprised him.

The warrior looked him over with an appraising eye. 'Good clothes, and jewellery concealed beneath, I'll wager.' He wagged the knife. 'Your effects should buy me a good baked byrnie and sword, and make a gentleman of me.' He began to move forward, menacingly.

And Gwent's calm broke: the huge anticlimax of being robbed and killed at this point was an impertinence he didn't intend to let the universe get away with: he leapt forward, brushing aside a tentative lunge, and then the in-fighting techniques he had been taught in the Movement took over. It was all too much for the warrior, who had obviously expected abject behaviour on the part of his victim; in seconds, Gwent's fingers tightened about his throat, clutching with a wild pressure. Gwent found himself longing to strangle the life of his man, as if to work off the fears and frustrations of the time he had spent in this new world. Instead, when the eyeballs seemed on the point of starting from the head, he unceremoniously dumped the would-be thief on the turf. The other still held the knife, and Gwent bent to take it from him. It was some kind of ceramic, he noted, and as he stood there, examining it, he realized that the language he had been answered in hadn't been English. Nor, for that matter, the language he himself had used. He scowled with annoyance. Was life under the magenta facetted sky to be an interminable procession of double-takes?

'Your name?'

'Wulf, sir.'

'Nationality?'

'English.'

Gwent made a wild guess: 'The year?'

'The Year of Our Lord One Thousand and Sixty Nine.'

Gwent tried to put time travel into the mélange of events and make a pattern, but none came. This new world became stranger the more one learned of it. This language they were both using with perfect familiarity – to his mind, it seemed like English, and it was a good bet that to Wulf it seemed like late Anglo Saxon: it fitted both like a perfect semantic glove. Wulf moved, and Gwent moved the knife forward.

'Go on,' Wulf said, fearfully. 'It's what we're here for.'

Gwent backed off a pace, still holding the knife out.

'You know what we're here for?'

'It's obvious.'

'Not to me.'

Wulf looked quite surprised, but volunteered no further information. Gwent felt himself growing impatient: this could go on all day, if that was the right word. He leant forward, almost jabbing the other in the face with the knife.

'Where are we?'

'In Hell, of course,' the beaten man said, as if shocked at having to say it. 'Where else?'

It was night, of a sort. And there were stars, of a sort. The vertices of the milliard facets glowed balefully out of the green; it was as bright as a new moon night. Wulf slept soundly; he was happy enough, now; he had refound his true vocation. He had been a thane's servant, dispossessed of his master in the New England, and mortally wounded in the Harrowing of the North. How he had come here was a little vague to him.

Gwent smiled to himself. He had met a real, live Anglo Saxon, and he found himself with particular interest in the fact. There was no question on that score he wanted to ask: the differences were small, human, accidental, of no account. The only important question was on the nature of this . . . device, that they both occupied. Wulf could believe it to be Hell, if he chose; but his new servant was hardly well informed. He would have brooded more, but he fell asleep.

Morning came with a tropical suddenness. The green spotted grey of the fell was brighter than it should be under the red arch of the facetted heavens. Wulf called it the Fell of Transfiguration, a hard place, and advised against seeking help in the houses whose smoke floated wispily to the sky every half mile or so. 'It's too easy to die under someone else's roof.' Although he was the willing servant, in the question of their destination he had been the master. 'There's nowhere else to go.'

What precisely the Folk Field was, Gwent had difficulty in deciding; direct questions yielded the answer that it was a field of people, camped out, but Wulf fought shy of revealing for what purpose. When Gwent asked if there were no cities, Wulf blanched like a maiden and begged him to be silent on that, here on the fells.

He did gather that they were people of Wulf's time at the Folk Field.

'There are priests there,' Wulf admitted. 'Some think we're in Hell, and some for lack of pains think we're in Purgatory, and there's one, Piers, that denied his faith. There's no bishop to settle the matter between them.' He paused. 'We may be in Hell, but it's sinful to despair, so I act as if I weren't.'

It was in the late afternoon – according to Wulf – when they saw the running man.

5

The Field of Folk spilled out on both sides of the river. Hrunting had seen such gatherings before, and never had the consequences been happy. His first thought was to ease his scramasax in its small scabbard, and to move his money supply to a safer concealment. He wondered whether there were any other Travellers here – and whether, this time, he might escape notice as one himself.

He was bringing his mind to the purpose of the gathering – of perhaps two or three thousand souls – when he saw a figure detach itself from the collage of tents and huts and screens, coming out across the rich valley land to meet him. He didn't vary his pace, but rested his hand on the hilt of his scramasax.

After they had moved for several minutes, he could make out that the figure was in a rough and ready priestly garb. His hand rested on the hilt of the scramasax still: the primary catchment area of this sector was the English Eleventh Century, and he knew it, and its priests, only too well.

'Welcome, brother,' the priest said. 'I am Father Piers.'

Hrunting nodded introducing himself with his new name.

'Are you come to join the Great Venture?'

Hrunting smiled: it was to be a great theft. 'I know nothing of it.'

It was the priest's turn to smile. 'It is my profession to dispel ignorance, brother. Our city has refused us access to the Gate. Even the sick and dying . . .'

'So?'

'So we take what is rightfully ours.'

'And the city?'

'One with Sodom and Gomorrah.'

164

Shouting, Wulf scurried off in search of non-existent cover, taking the knife with him. Gwent looked about, as if for help of some kind, but there was no help against the running man. Gwent stood his ground and waited a short eternity while the green clad figure of the running man drew near. This was a fighting man he could see: the green was not clothing, but some kind of armour; it encased him like a knight's plate armour in the dying days of chivalry, but it in no way impeded him. When he was so close that Gwent could see grey eyes peering out of the green, the runner gracefully extracted with his right hand a glittering gold ceramic sword, and a silver gleaming ceramic misericorde with his left.

Gwent felt a sudden panic. Was it to be death at this man's hands for enmities not his, and with so much to learn? No! He stripped off his jacket, and, holding it by the collar, waited. Without change of pace, the running man came at him. Gwent noticed how the armour moved with him, like a second skin. When they were five yards apart, he flung the jacket. As if mechanically, the running man slashed at it, but it tangled on his misericorde, and made him mistime the sword stroke. Gwent's muscles remembered the long hours spent at combat judo in seedy backrooms, and he caught the arm on the down swing, gripping it with both hands. He swung it up and sideways, kicking himself backwards as he did so. The green runner jerked into the air, out of Gwent's grip, to crumple on the turf three yards away.

Gwent had gone back too hard, winded himself. He could vaguely make out the green runner stirring, but his body refused to do anything about it. He'd almost won; he couldn't give up now. He rolled on to his face, gasping for breath, and pushed himself up on his arms. But it was unnecessary. Wulf stood over his opponent, brandishing his own knife. The green runner made an ineffectual one-armed grab – the other arm was broken – at the servant, for both his weapons had spun beyond his reach, but Wulf was quick. He jumped out of reach, only to dive back, the knife darting for the unprotected eyes, once, twice, and then deep.

Gwent eased himself back to the earth, not watching. Even dying, the green runner maintained that almost inhuman silence.

Gwent finally struggled to his feet. Wulf paused a moment in his stripping of the dead man.

'My lord, no one else at Folk Field has a harness of living armour. You'll truly be a great man, a leader.' He turned back to the delicate job of stripping the now limp, green harness from its bloody-faced former owner, only adding casually: 'Serving you will be an honourable estate.'

PART TWO: TO THE CITY

I

'HERE, there are no coincidences . . .'

Hrunting's words, uttered in passing to him just before the strategy meeting he was currently enduring, haunted Gwent; they were like a key he had been casually handed, but without the location of the appropriate door, or a hint as to what lay beyond it.

'. . . and so, if I may summarize our resolutions?' The Elder paused to brush back his long, white-blond hair and let his glance play over the council of the Folk Field, squatting before him in the makeshift council tent. The question was pro forma: he reflected the general will of the meeting too accurately and too forcefully for there to be any dissent. 'So, the assault which I shall lead, with Traveller Gwent accompanying me, shall in its earlier stages be a decoy only: the city is impregnable from the landward side alone. We have, therefore, accepted Traveller Hrunting's plan for an attack from the sea, which he has graciously consented to aid my daughter in leading . . .' The Elder's words droned on, and Gwent felt himself drawn in against his will into this petty struggle, with aims he scarcely understood. He was a little amazed at being accorded the title, 'Traveller', which seemingly was the due of Hrunting and, from what he could gather, of all those who had passed more Gates than those of initial transfiguration.

No coincidences. What did Hrunting mean by that? There was the matter of the citizen who had, apparently co-incidentally, donated the superb harness of living armour he now wore. (He had had it stained a decent red.) Wulf had explained how it worked – it was a plant that lived sym-biotically with him, on him, his sweat and evacuations, and the idea had appalled at first. After three weeks it no longer did so: he knew that when he peeled it off, he would be cleaner than ever before in his life, his skin as clean as a surgeon's fresh gloves. And his new hide was tough: it could take a sword thrust without penetration. But the running man, alone on the fell . . .

The meeting was winding up: the leaders of the Folk Field, earthy people in drab garments, were getting to their feet as quickly as their rheumatic limbs were able, readying them-selves to shuffle back beneath the hellish sky to their tents four hundred yards away, across the heather. Gwent had no wish to join them: he rose from his squat and stalked arro-gantly to the North, where the dim shapes of the high fells jutted upwards at the sunless sky.

After a while, he was aware of rustlings in the heather: he was being followed. But the nature of the rustlings reassured him, and he kept his hands from his two swords, and went on to the base of the flint-dark outcropping. She joined him there.

Gwent looked at her, at her long, light brown hair draping the shoulders of her sheer, white dress, and tried to analyse the emotions she roused in him. Love? – an overblown word; he wasn't about to go and slay dragons for her. Or was he? Was she the reason he'd allowed himself to be ensnared into this war? Her feelings for him were more obvious: even meeting him here was not quite in keeping with the mores of the valley farmers who made up the Folk Field.

'You are troubled,' she said, in a kind of Middle English. She always eschewed the use of Gate Language with him, and he understood her well enough. But his attempts to use that language puzzled and amused her: it was hard to re-member which commonplace words were old, and which had been coined in the centuries that separated their speech.

'The fighting . . .'

'You are not afraid.'

He smiled: it was not wholly true, but she was so firm, he agreed. 'It's just that, sometimes, I wonder if I've picked the right side. From all accounts, the city has a very advanced biotechnology.' He paused, then descended to tautology: 'In fine, they seem to be more civilized.'

'At our expense!' she flared. 'Do you think they made all that: they found it! For many years, they were content to trade with us in the valley, to let the old and sick and Travellers use the Gate – but now they've gone mad. Was the citizen whose suit you wear more civilized than we, who have welcomed you to our homes?'

Her anger made her beautiful, and he toned down his objection until it faded away into meaninglessness. But all the time, his mind was working overtime: the citizens had *found* their city. So who had made it? Not for the first time in these past weeks, he was appalled at the extent of his ignorance. He had drained Wulf dry of knowledge and fable. Jehane's father, the Elder, and his clique of major farmers, were a little better informed than the common run; but their preoccupations were economic, not philosophical. Hrunting the Traveller could tell him more; but he was strangely reluctant to do so.

The sky was changing: a faint greenish cast could be seen: night was at hand. He looked into Jehane's waiting, deep, dark eyes. And he was afraid, afraid for her, for she would accompany Hrunting's party – as if she were the Elder's son, for the valley people would not follow even this Hrunting of the Many Names and fabled reputation without such a gesture. But surely he would see her safe. He was truly afraid of something else, of forming attachments, putting roots into this artificial soil. It would be so easy!

'We'd better be getting back,' he said, avoiding her eyes.

2

Hrunting was not happy about the meeting. It was inevitable, he realized, but he liked the idea none the better for that. Tact was not one of his strong points. Of course, Gwent was a Traveller; even the ciphers could see that. That potential might be delayed in realization, especially if the Elder's daughter had her way, but not forever. And new Travellers should be allowed to bring their own insights to the Great Problem, and not be given the accepted ideas too quickly.

'Where?' he temporized. 'I suppose that's the question you've come to ask.'

'Among others.'

'Where do you think?' Hrunting looked hard at him: he was not a handsome man; there was a coldness in his grey eyes, and a hardness in his features: an archetypal villain! Also, rather like a younger version of himself.

'It's a thing, isn't it?'

'Res extensa, res cogitans – the difference seems profound, but in fact is subtle and not helpful. If we live in a dream, technological or spiritual, the question still is – whose?'

Gwent seemed scarcely to hear. 'It's a device!'

Hrunting smiled. This was turning out easier than he had expected. 'That's the accepted view, but we lack confirmation.'

'We?'

'The Fellowship of Travellers – it's not an organized band, but we know each other, and others know us, however much we try to be inconspicuous. And we help each other.' He paused. 'We travel the Gates, not when we're dying and afraid like the ciphers, but with a purpose – to learn the purpose of the Gates, and the sectors they join, and of their makers. We chart them through dozens of metalless worlds like this, and all the Gates we've found are looped together, with the furthest forward catchment area in the 21st century. Our aim is to break through this loop, so we may know the purpose of Manganon.'

'Manganon?'

Hrunting smiled again, briefly. 'It's an old word, and it means "device".'

'And I'm one of you?'

'You will be.' Hrunting spoke now with absolute assurance. 'But first I'm going to tell you why you're going to fight. Not through simple inertia, or for an Elder's daughter:

but because the city controls a Gate.' He paused dramatically. 'An uncharted Gate.'

Afterwards, Hrunting felt a little guilty. The Gate wasn't in Travellers' Tales, so in that sense he had spoken the truth; but it could hardly be uncharted with a Magister Portarum in residence, and he knew there was one, he could feel the draw of one, subtle and impossible to pinpoint, but there with a surety one couldn't doubt. But it had been the right thing to do. Gwent had to learn for himself, as he had done. It hadn't been hard, of course, to cut the flow of questions. He'd used the old and trusted trick of Travellers, and casually answered the patently unasked question.

'You realize,' he'd said, almost offhandedly, 'that by travelling the great Gates, we become, effectively, immortal?'

3

It was time. Hrunting had no watch – in all Manganon there were no watches – but like all Travellers he had a sense of time, necessarily. He rubbed his eyes and slipped from the vegfoam bunk, reaching out to touch the closed sphincter that served the half-alive cabin as a port hole. At his touch, the sphincter slowly opened, with all the grace of a flower opening under a dawn sun, dispelling the green gloom as it opened on the blood red midday sky.

The surface of the sea was covered, as ever, with the omnipresent sungreen: the tideless ocean was like one vast Sargasso. In the distance he could just make out the coast with the imposing vegmuscle structure of the City drawn up on it like an abandoned ship: which perhaps was not too far from the truth.

He grew aware of the ache in his left arm and found himself half-wishing he'd accepted Gwent's offer of his living suit. But the barge had been successfully, if painfully, taken, providing them with living suits in plenty, and now there was little chance of Gwent dying uselessly in the taking of the City.

The City was an old problem, much dealt with in Traveller's Tales, being found in many guises in many Gate sectors. The problem was, why did *they* allow such high levels of biotechnology, when they effectively banned any significant level of conventional technology by making Manganon completely metalless, except for trace elements?

The usual answer was the blanket selection answer: that Manganon was a device for selecting the best and the fittest, for some unknown purpose, and guns and bombs were too indiscriminate as a means to that end. There were suspicions as to what that purpose was: the abuttal of the concepts of entropy and time travel leading to the hugest project capable of conception; but like all hypotheses in Manganon, it was wild, unconfirmed ... How could it be confirmed, when *they* were as silent as the maker of Paley's watch?

But now was no time for speculation. Hrunting quickly donned the suit of living armour, grown of the same living vegmuscle as ship and City, opened the large sphincter of the door with a touch, climbed through and walked the length of the orange leaf corridor to where grew the spiral staircase that led down to the upper deck.

He burst into the brightness of the deck, half expecting to be met by some of the boarding party, but there was none, and he looked leisurely about him. The barge consisted of a vast, flat-topped hull of vegmuscle which sucked water and sungreen in at the prow, and with a spasm of its internal chamber, jetted the water out at the stern. A system of filters extracted the sungreen on the way, to be used as food for the whole structure, the hull, the upper decks at stern and prow, and the whole elaborate panoply of rooms, small holds and minor decks that surmounted the upper decks in ragged pyramids.

The barge almost looked like a natural thing, a freak of nature rather than a biological artifact. He was beginning to appreciate the subtle artistry of the colours. At first, he had only noted how the deep chlorophyll green of the hull gave way to rising, lighter shades, variegated with tiny splashes of orange and red; now he felt the pattern. However crude the citizens might be politically, they had no peers in the art of growing ships and cities.

On the walkway thirty yards below, there was more colour and movement: Jehane in a green and orange living suit. She was on her way to join him, and she would need careful handling. Rumour had it that Gwent had rebuffed her, and he certainly didn't want to be her target on the rebound. A Traveller could not love and remain a Traveller, and he was deep set in his ways. It was, in fact, an embarrassment having a woman on such a venture, but thankfully, she seemed competent enough. Whether she was or not, the ship would be in her hands when he led the crucial assault.

'All's well?'

She nodded. 'Everyone knows their parts. There's just the fear that we should make some recognition signal as we enter harbour . . .'

That was it. There was some reassurance to be gained from the consideration that never before had a ship been taken, or even attacked. That was what had made the assault on the Northern Outpost so easy and cheap in lives: ships were useless to the valley people: the city's colonies traded only with the city.

'We can safely discount that.' He smiled, reassuringly, and was suddenly personally aware of her beauty. Ciphers we call them, he thought, because they are content simply to live, while we must explore and quest endlessly; perhaps we are truly the ciphers. His eyes dwelt a moment on the peach skin of her face – all that the suit revealed – almost envying Gwent his chance. After a moment, he averted his gaze, and forced the thoughts down: he was too deep set in his ways.

Seen from the sea, the City was a green horse-shoe, both ends jutting into the sea itself. Between them, separated from them by the glaucous water, rose a tall island of green veg-muscle, and this was connected by the narrow umbilical of bridge to the citadel tower that rose, a third, but vertical prong from the very centre of the City's seaward wall. Perhaps other arteries and veins ran beneath the sea's surface, through the huge suction pad by means of which the City clung to the coast, all now hidden by the opacity of the slimy ocean.

The City grew large, enormous, dwarfing even the great

barge they rode in, its matt green yielding to a chromatic symphony of blending greens, a creation of breath taking beauty that they were about to steal, and perhaps destroy in the act of stealing.

The barge, its biological engine pumping at maximum pulse, veered close to the sheer walled island of vegmuscle that served the City as heart and breakwater. The steersman, and Jehane, who now commanded him, were navigating well. But Hrunting had other things to think of – of the assault team who stood with him at the pinnacle of the barge's top-heavy superstructure, of what to say to them. He looked over the thirty faces. They were expressionless. He considered a short, rousing-speech, and it died still-born in his throat. They had all been carefully instructed. There was nothing to do now but wait, and fight, and hope.

Already the citizens had sensed the wrongness. Several times they heard the whistle of stone chips shuttering above their heads from the mangonels of City and island. Hrunting looked again at the assault party and noticed Piers among them, a godless priest with a face of carpentered wood ... The barge was slowing. The low part of the bridge near the island loomed below: if it held and did not shear!

Slower and slower the barge glided. Finally came the impact, the superstructure cutting into and through the hollow bridge with a savage, tearing sound of ruptured veg-muscle. The mangonel barrage became particularly intense: chips buried themselves in the half-living but unfeeling veg-muscle. Hrunting didn't heed it. Now! he thought – and leapt from the sagging tatters of the barge's superstructure down on to the slippery, curved surface of the broken bridge. The bridge shook as the stream of concentrated sungreen, the life-giving sap of the City, jetted uselessly down over the maltreated superstructure of the barge.

He lost his secondary sword, needing the hand that held it to steady himself on the swaying, seawet surface; but he held on. The rest of the assault party overcame their difficulties with like determination.

The stone chips hailed at them in a constant stream now, but only from the citadel; the heart island's mangonel couldn't be brought to bear. Hrunting looked about him; on the faces of the assault party, sternness was yielding to stark fear. How best to impel them to action? An impassioned harangue. No. There was only one way.

'For the Gate!' he screamed, and began to race down the truncated stump of the bridge for the heart island.

He heard the sound of movement behind, and looked back to see the ciphers running wild-eyed in his wake. Behind them, the great ship was alive again, her jet beating up the waters to a fine frenzy as it forced the longer element of the bridge away at an angle. If a repair of the bridge could be effected, the island could be reinforced, and they were dead. Otherwise . . .

But he had no time for speculation. His men were about him now, and he greeted them with a grandiloquent onward motion of his sword. An unspent chip caught him in the right upper arm; he almost dropped his sword, but the long training of his youth told, and he ran on, forcing the pain out of his mind, and with it, almost everything else but the urge to give battle.

The bridge gave on to a downward stairway at the island end. He took the stairs by the half dozens, almost falling at the end; but he was on his feet when he was confronted in the well of the stairway. The wattle-faced man swung at him wildly. He parried the blow in the high line, recovered with practised ease and struck at the pale oval of his opponent's face with arm-wrenching force. The blow bit through cartilage and bone; the citizen jerked, then fell like an abandoned puppet, splaying his limbs.

Now he was no longer in the lead. Assault group ciphers had flowed about him as he fought, down along the corridor that led to the heart chamber stairway. He followed them. At the head of the stairway he paused; he could make out the sounds of fighting, the raspings, grunts and smothered curses as both sides clawed for dominance in the life-generated flourescence of the heart chamber, and the spaced-out bursts of the tin-can rattling of knife and sword work, terminating in screams.

Inevitably, he leapt down the stairway, avoiding a pair of broken legs only by the best good fortune. A thrown knife bedded in the vegmuscle nearby, perhaps flung in haste by one of his own side from the position they held behind the tendon posts, where the white-green tendons that regulated the spasm of the city's heart chamber were fixed to their controlling levers. Sense told him to take cover; impulse sent him in full fury at the nearest citizen hiding behind one of the unused ceramic posts. The citizen, unarmoured, twisted fearfully about to face this new challenge. He parried Hrunting's first blow, but not well enough; deflected, it severed the left upper arm, and the citizen fell, his stumped arm issuing blood in great, pulsing gouts.

Hrunting paid him no further attention. A sword swished past his own ear, and he heard a screech of agony that could only have come from one of his own men. Ignoring it, he ran on, wielding the sword like a meat cleaver, drinking the heady mélange of blood, fear and death about him, exulting in it, yet knowing with some remaining sane element of his mind that afterwards, if he lived, he would despise himself for this indulgence.

Suddenly, he caromed against one of the tendon posts, slipping in blood he had shed. A green shape loomed – an armoured citizen. Hrunting's sword was struck from his hand; a blade, reflecting the odd white of the tendons, swung at him. So they must finally still the heart without him. He hardly felt afraid, just curious: how would it feel when it bit . . . ?

4

The Elder was the handsome father of a handsome daughter, and accoutred as he was, as a warrior, ready to give the signal for Gwent to lead the first attack, he held all eyes. But Gwent's eyes unwillingly: the vast bulk of the green ramp that led to the open city portal, with the over-scaled frieze brooding over ramp and portal, lured them to fleeting, fearful glances.

The watcher stationed by the coast lowered his arms. That meant he could no longer see the barge: it was in the harbour. The Elder shouted. Gwent started like a hare, racing up the ramp, half the young blood of the valley people behind him, racing to be in front.

Out of his eye corners, Gwent could see them draw level with him, all sword waving and fury. His own sword stayed firmly scabbarded: if all went well, there would be no use for it. The great portal drew closer; he could see quite clearly the flower-like heads that made up the detail of the frieze; he saw them move, braced himself. And suddenly he was running into the wall of sea that issued from them, and water was all over him, crushing the air from his lungs; he was drowning – and then, just as suddenly, he was lying with a small host of others on the ramp, wet, winded, dead if the citizens chose to counter-attack. But with the bulk of the army still untouched, no counter-attack spilled screaming through the portal.

Wearily, he got to his feet, looking at the tempting, open portal with a kind of hate. It was a trap. There was positively no way past that wall of water. If Hrunting had failed . . .

The Elder was signalling again. This was the full attack. Gwent motioned his still dripping men onward, drawing his own sword this time. They had scarcely managed more than a few paces when the water again struck them. But without quite the previous violence. Digging their swords in the rubbery ramp, they held their places. Slowly they continued their upward passage. The water struck a third time; but the force of it had ebbed. The heart of the city had been broken! The main body of the army was screaming its charge, and Gwent impelled his own men upwards, faster and faster – so they would escape being impaled on the weapons of their rearward comrades.

Then they were through the portal, a toll taken of them by a flight of arrows, one bouncing harmlessly off his living suit, past the flaccid petals of the frieze of water into the bloody, mindless business of hand to hand fighting. Citizens and valley people alike slid into the redder, hazier waters of psychogenetic rage . . .

PART THREE: THE GATE

I

HE WAS dying: it was no new sensation. He tried to open his eyes, but only pain sprang at his consciousness. He held on, and, gradually, the memory of a sword slashing down at the only unprotected part of him – his face – came to mind. He no longer had eyes. The question was: had he a face? He moved his lips, forced out a word.

'There?'

There was an answer of some kind, but it dissolved in a miasma of pain. A moment or an eternity later, he spoke again. The pain was less this time.

'Who?'

'Gwent.'

'Ah . . .' It was a sigh of relief. The city was taken: there was a Gate for him. Before him, only the little death of the Gate . . .

Gwent looked down on what had been wrought with a dulled horror. His sword had wrought as much and worse only hours before. Jehane knelt and dabbed at the mangled redness, and he walked away, to the window, whence he could see the wreck of the great bridge, the longer remnant swaying gently in the sea breeze. He stood there a long time, the lassitude of battle won leadening his limbs.

He felt his arm being taken. He half turned and saw Jehane's face, caught in the window light, all grace and beauty caught in an instant of time. The instant lengthened into a moment, a duration; it could stretch into a lifetime, ruling this city with her; unbidden, his mind began to picture it. Then the weak voice of Hrunting ended the moment.

'An end to entropy . . .'

For a moment again, the words seemed without meaning, and then things began to fall in place in Gwent's mind, the hints, the nuances, the half completed assertions. Entropy, time travel, Manganon . . . A passing thought: the words spoken no longer mattered: he knew. Manganon was the creation of eternity! He knew it – not how, or why, or by whom, but *what*!

Jehane knew: not the fantastic idea blossoming in his mind, but of her danger of losing him. He could see it in her eyes. She was like nothing in the primary world, he thought suddenly; and he realized how distanced everything there was, had been from the beginning. Had the Gate of Transfiguration done more than he had suspected? Or hadn't all that blood and soil ranting, street fighting and the easy, amoral cameraderie of the Movement really mattered much to him? Just a way of easing boredom under the New Order? Was she just another, passing comrade? His hand brushed her cheek, tentatively then tenderly.

Then Hrunting moaned again, piteously, and she was drawn back to her charge. As she knelt over the wounded Traveller, Gwent slipped silently out of the room.

Wulf, resplendent in an apple green living suit, awaited beyond the sphincter door.

'The Gate!'

Wulf nodded, and led him down dim green corridors that towards the end, in sight of the huge flap door, were littered with refuse and offal. In the chamber, beyond the door, there was more, but seemingly without smell – the citizens had been excellent bio-engineers.

In the centre of the chamber, as if sculpted from the veg-muscle of the floor, was a deep green flower, slightly speckled over with red; from petal to petal it was larger than a man, but the indentations were shallow, and gave it an ornamental aspect.

The citizens were grouped about the flower in a great inward shuffling spiral, tired men, naked now of their armour, their eyes almost dead. The guards, just as tired, but obviously exultant in bizarre compromises of their own and living armour, prodded the unfortunates, moving the spiral inward. One prisoner was almost upon the flower centre of the chamber.

'We have to pass this way,' Wulf said, almost guiltily.

A guard ran to the prisoner nearest the flower, gestured at it with his sword. The prisoner looked at the sword, then at the flower, and spoke softly in the silence.

> 'Crystal splintered,
> shards glittering fell;
> hoarse the screaming day
> welcomed night's advent:
> the city panted:
> living gods were sundered:
> the green bridge
> veining with black
> folded into the silent torrent . . .'

The guard smiled, made to jab the man with his sword, but the prisoner anticipated him, and stepped on to the inset petals of the flower.

Gwent, whose arms were still rimed with the blood of citizens, whose arms ached with slashing into their flesh, froze with horror. For, unhurriedly, the flower ate the man.

Slowly, with infinite delicacy and grace the petals did their work and for the most part of a dilated minute, Gwent was held rigid by the horror of it, towards the end, what remained of the man over the reddening petals uttered a small cry, and Gwent grasped his sword hilt, whether to end the man's sufferings or begin those of his murderer, he had no idea. But whatever his intention, enough of it was divined to frustrate it all. The strong arms of Wulf engulfed him in a bear hug.

'No, master. The Elder ordered this.'

The grip eased, and, unprotesting, Gwent was led on through the chamber – one of the city's refuse disposal chambers, he realized with sudden clarity – as the process continued.

> '. . . the crack-faced gods,
> despoiled of their sublimity,
> wither to their stone shells:
> like animals submit
> the former images of man . . .'

The words themselves died as new flap doors closed behind them; but they lingered in his mind a few moments longer: there was something odd about them. For a moment, he thought they were English, an odd, clipped English with a strange intonation, but it was easy enough to mistake Gate Language for one's primary tongue. Yes, that was it; had to be.

Sunlight was a rebirth, its warmth a benediction: it faded the reds and browns of trauma into a soft beige, soon to be dissolved in the Lethe waters of Sanity.

Distanced – by space, or the fury of battle – the citadel tower rose imposing; now, seen from its plaza, the towering green height and the smooth green bulk of its curving surface was an imposition, a blow between the eyes. Gwent stared at it, wondering at the men who had built this city, in whose wanton destruction he was playing a part.

Whump! A mangonel stone crashed into the citadel's base, and then another, and another, all into the same place, which in no way betrayed any signs of a door; they all bounced off without causing any obvious damage. Gwent turned to see the Elder ordering a battery of mangonels at the perimeter of the plaza.

It had the air of a pointless exercise, but an unasked Wulf voiced a contrary opinion.

'We'll have it before sunset.'

The Elder was tired, bloody, sweaty. He still wore his own improvised armour, leathern jack and cap, and the sword that swung from his hip was his own. His eyes were harder than before, betraying a fixity of purpose Gwent had not suspected – although it had been obvious all along, he realized. It was as if he were seeing the Elder for the first time: the previous weeks since his transfiguration could have been a dream, with the world revolving around his consciousness. They had ended in nightmare, debouching him into reality.

The Elder greeted him, smiled at Wulf in his stolen armour, and looked back at the citadel.

'They built that over the Gate,' he said. 'They used to let our dying in, for the new life; then they went mad. Now we shall have that without their charity!'

The battering continued; the valley people slaved at the mangonels, forming human chains to bring stones to them, and Gwent just stood watching, feeling his apartness, and knowing wonder and horror and awe as he hedged about the idea Hrunting had half suggested, as if he were luring him into it by degrees, and near completed in his delirium. *Their* purpose.

Not necessarily the true purpose; but the one Travellers believed in: an end to entropy. Not as a doctrine of means, not in everyday affairs, but a doctrine of ends, a teleology, and perhaps, in its ramifications, a kind of theology.

Gwent felt suddenly tired of it all. The shiny newness had worn off things. He had had fantasies of ruling these people, or of becoming a Traveller and learning the secret of this pocket universe, but they had been fantasies in a fantasy – and suddenly there was no more fantasy left. He had killed, seen pain and death and sacrifice to this abomination of victory. More would die in the citadel. And the Travellers were other than he had believed. Here and now, this was reality; he had to accommodate himself to it, and there was a room he knew where someone tended the sick who could make that accommodation worthwhile.

The sun was setting when the concealed base sphincter's biological mechanism finally broke down under the bombardment, and the hordes burst through, silent now, but still ignorant of mercy.

PART FOUR: THE CASTE

I

IT WAS Father Piers who came to fetch them. It was past noon of the new day, and the window light caught his face, revealing a mixture of envy and bitterness as he spoke the words:

'We have found a Magister Portarum. You are to come, and bring Master Hrunting with you.'

Gwent saw stark fear in Jehane's face. He wanted to comfort her, but words wouldn't come, and he just nodded to the priest. Piers smiled bitterly, and Gwent now knew the cause of that bitterness: Travellers were the true priests of this world; they eschewed preaching, but it was they who sacrificed at the Gates.

The speaking of the Latin name seemed to give new life to the dying Hrunting. He climbed miraculously to his feet, and stood, precariously, waiting to be led. The bloody bandages on his face were already drying black.

'Shall we go?' said Piers, matter of factly.

The city had been cleaned up; but here and there were still traces of blood, and every so often, one saw the tired, furtive face of a city-born child, spared after the waning of the bloodlust, but enslaved.

After a few hundred yards Hrunting stumbled and together they had to carry him – awkwardly. But they were already at the plaza. It had not been completely cleared: around the base of the citadel, bodies were stacked, still in their living suits, suits already bloated and loathsome from feasting on the corpses they enwrapped.

The sphincter had jammed open. None had known how to repair it, and that would be the way of it, Gwent realized. The conquerors would live in the now heartless city for a year or two, not repairing it, or even tending it, and it would die, street by street, and one by one the valley people would drift back to their farms and homesteads, until finally only the Gate was guarded, and desolation reigned.

They went down a spiral stairway, into the gloom, and then at Father Piers' touch of an unidentified section of the wall a small sphincter opened, and the Gate glowed behind it. Piers avoided even glancing inside, but stalked back the way he had come.

The Gate itself was only a point in space, but points need pointing out – by a plaque, or an arrow painted in red on a brown wall, or as in this case, by a chair. A throne, more aptly. At first, Gwent thought it was an exception to this metalless world: a frame of gold and silver, once dipped in a tub of jewels, but closer inspection revealed it as even more remarkable. It was a single plant, and the colours were soft, butterfly colours, but glittering and glinting as if the energies of the Gate shone through. Perhaps they did.

'Pretty, eh?'

Gwent looked into the shadowed corner of the room, and made out the face of a man – the Magister Portarum.

'Yes,' he answered simply

'A pretty trinket, no more.' The Magister Portarum stepped out into the light, and Gwent saw a youth before him, in a dark one piece suit, just like a living suit, but of simple material.

'So you are Gwent.' The youth smiled; but it was not the smile of a young man, and neither was his voice. Both hinted at vast experience; this man had held power for generations, Gwent's intuition told him, for all that appearances were to the contrary; it was an intuition he trusted.

The youth watched him, his eyes seeming to divine his thoughts. Perhaps they did. Finally the Magister Portarum broke the developing silence.

'Put Hrunting in the chair.'

Gwent obeyed, carefully easing the now scarcely conscious man into the delicate tracery of life that the other dismissed as a mere bauble. Gwent felt cold fear, expecting the Traveller to disappear before his eyes, but he merely sprawled. The Magister Portarum laughed.

'Axon Gates are subtle, unlike the Dendrite Gate you passed through. There are degrees of interpenetration, and control, for those who learn how to exercise it.'

He paused, then: 'Of course, you are a Traveller, although you scarcely know what one is, or grows to be, which is why Hrunting remains: two Travellers are formally necessary for an induction. But first, you have some guesses?'

Gwent was beginning to find this knowing, utterly self confident seeming-youth annoying, very annoying. He had been too well anticipated, so he decided to try another tack.

'The guards who were in here, with you. You stopped them from using the Gate?'

'Am I responsible for the stacked corpses without? In a sense, yes – but not in the sense you mean. I encouraged them to go through, begged even, and for all the respect they bore me, not inconsiderable, they scarcely listened.

'I am the author of this destruction – but only because I had no other choice. The city went mad; it turned away from its Gate, and the chance of eternal life, retreating into a dream, the old heresy, that this is a variant of the primary world, and can be lived in as such.'

'It's a way station?'

'Less – a filter.'

Hrunting groaned in the chair. The Magister Portarum looked at him, and for a moment the shape of the wounded Traveller seemed to blur, then return to reality, and the sprawling was no longer born of weariness and pain, but a relaxing of the spirit.

Gwent's annoyance faded too, and he realized the significance of the words the Magister Portarum had just used: filter, axon and dendrite. He had compared this ... sector with a nerve cell that received information by several incoming pathways – dentrites – integrated them chemically, then passed the integrated message on through a solitary channel, the axon. A nerve cell – also a brain cell. Gwent didn't proceed far with the thought, but far enough to see the implications of such an analogy, indeterminate, diffuse, overwhelming.

'I have seen a hundred sectors,' the seeming-youth said, 'like small universes all of them, and ciphers in them more than half believing them so. The human mind is very conservative; evolution in millions of years in the primary is not brushed away like cobwebs from a stairway. So people and cities reject their Gates; Tithonus rejected immortality without eternal youth of the body: real people reject eternal youth of the body if it doesn't bring with it eternal youth of the mind. Form without renewal.' He smiled, wanly. 'But you were about to tell me of your guesses.'

'Manganon is the creation of eternity,' Gwent heard himself saying, and the Magister Portarum smiled again, and began to speak, softly, persistently, using Gate language, but heightened in some way, so that it seemed to impinge directly on Gwent's consciousness, a great dialectic of gaudy, fragile butterfly wing images capped by a synthesis of Heisenbergian indeterminacy. And through this, Gwent saw *them*, felt what they felt when the anentropic phenomenon of time travel showed *them* the end of the singular outfolding and infolding of energy that was the universe and that ylem barrier to human progression, and felt the pointlessness of it all, in that it would end, and felt with *them* the surge of *their* spirits as he was shown how it could be, how the past could be drained of energy to maintain expansion until the last witness quasar hid behind the curtain of light, and beyond to the age of iron, and beyond, when mankind inhabited a universe of dying dwarfs and Schwarzchild singularities and beyond again, until the tail of the snake was eaten, and mankind must resolve its problems anew.

And he knew the why of Manganon, knew it for the cage it was to ciphers and the maze it became to Travellers, who would go on to make this be.

The Magister Portarum stopped talking: the spell broke, and Gwent found himself breathing hard, as if he had been engaged on the hardest work.

'I offer no proof,' the Magister Portarum said. 'What I say, I offer more as a myth than a hypothesis . . .'

'A myth . . .' Gwent began, uttering sceptical words utterly without scepticism: '. . . has vague beginnings.'

'And yet, Travellers believe it, and have believed it through a thousand transfigurations, the only meaningful way to compute time. If you designed this . . . Manganon, for a purpose, and rumours circulated in it that were at cross purposes to your purpose, wouldn't you end them? Don't doubt that *they* have the power to do it. But mightn't they even start them?'

'Which would be no guarantee of their truth.' The words surprised Gwent; how could he doubt?

'Precisely,' the Magister Portarum said, 'and if the truth were too great, one would start with little truths, building towards the great truth.'

Gwent knew he was caught, trapped into a grand design and he could be either an unwilling tool or a believing disciple. Whichever, he already had the gift of immortality, and then the choice was made, and not even the shadow of a shadow of doubt remained: he believed.

'You are inducted,' the Magister Portarum said formally, and Gwent saw that Hrunting was no longer in the chair. Now its tracery glowed invitingly at him.

'There's all the time in eternity,' the Magister Portarum said kindly. 'Go back – live, rule here if you can, until you can bear it no longer. The Gate is always waiting.'

Part Five: Magister Portarum

The Magister Portarum – he had no need or use for any other name – watched Gwent leave, abstractedly. Gwent didn't interest him particularly: he had inducted many Travellers, and Gwent was scarcely exceptional. He would take a few years in this sector still, and it would be many transfigurations then before he would add significantly to the great book of Travellers' Tales, and his copy, carried in his head, for memory was the only commodity that could be taken by axon transfiguration from sector to sector, would grow slowly, building the sustaining myth.

And how many more years would he, the Magister Portarum, have to wait before a Traveller of sufficient seniority and experience transfigured all unknowing into this sector, for unwelcome promotion? A year, a century – time was not of the essence. But truth was.

How much of it had he told Gwent? He looked at the chair, and where the chair was, looked through it, at the Gate. Some Travellers saw only an emptiness, tugging reality into it; ciphers and young Travellers saw nothing at all; but he saw such beauty as scarce his mind could hold. Truth, beauty – beauty, truth; and by way of a very devious and tortuous argument, the benignity of *them*. There was a whole philosophy built on that premise, but not one the Magister Portarum cared for.

He had told Gwent no knowing lies. Gwent would believe, and believing he would have a foundation to build on, later, to question and qualify. There was much for him to learn, carefully placed clues he had failed to appreciate – how he, the Magister Portarum, in the fastness of the city had bent first the Elder and then the ciphers to his will; how he had brought the rook of Hrunting into that game, and the knight of Gwent. And that most intriguing of all problems, the lack of coincidence in Manganon; one could call it the lack of synchronicity or seriality, but it boiled down to the fact that in Manganon, bell shaped curves used descriptively were always, painfully, perfectly bell shaped.

Except when a Magister Portarum worked his will, the universe of Manganon was strictly causal: the diagonal of acausality that blurred the edges in the primary world didn't exist here, save in an attenuated form about the Axon Gates.

For a moment, he thought of his city people, his devoted city people who still had dammed the flow to the Axon, and of what had been — yes, the passive was the best way to express it — done to them. But only for a moment. Then he let his private vision expand, out beyond the city walls, beyond the valley, past the limited discontinuities of Dendrite Gates into the regions where Manganon blurred into the dubious reality of the primary world.

Who was he? Oh, he could remember his past, if it were his; his Travellership, everything. But belief and memory and truth are not necessarily linked. Where do we end, and *they* begin?

In Manganon — a device, a thing, he told himself, but a fearful, transcendent, awesome, beautiful thing!

PART SIX: HERESIES

Travellers' Tales: being some of the better known aphorisms and assertions of the School of Itinerant Wisdom in the sector known as Inusyeyash, or Gaetor.

I

MARGENSTAERN: Our speech on such things is pointless. My esteemed colleague has paraphrased Mr. Dirac in saying that in one's ideas one should hold beauty more important than experiment. However, the originator of that assertion hardly envisaged a situation in which no experiment is possible.

GARNET: My colleague disposes of experiment merely because he can think of none.

MARGENSTAERN: Can you?

GARNET: Off the cuff, no. But I do not therefore deny the possibility of such experiment. You raise our limitations into an insuperable barrier to knowledge; I would sooner just raise them.

II

BENBABUN: The trouble with the general explanation is its overweening arrogance. *They* are not engaged on any small task. No. They are prolonging the life of the universe. You and I know very well that a great many of the fraternity of the Magistri Portarum actually believe that *they* by prolonging are also creating the universe. Do not be shocked! If you too believe in the 'Essential Mystery', then fear not to bring it into the light of day. So that we can see it for the farrago of misconceptions and simple fantasies that it is. It has the same proof as the basic, less elaborate theory from which it sprang: *they* permit us to believe it, so it must be essentially true.

Even *they* are an assumption. Only Manganon we know. But considering Manganon, *they* are a valid assumption. You ask me what is my explanation. I have no explanation, but if you wish me in indulge in speculation, I am willing to do so.

The purpose of Manganon. To save some sample of humanity. In the general fantasy, to prolong itself, the universe has to eat the energy of its historical tail. Manganon is outside time, but the Gates provide a kind of time and the progression through them a kind of evolution and history. We become *they* when *their* work has eaten *their* other ancestors. I'm sure an argument could be made that from us, *they* could get the same genetic endowment as from the whole of humanity. How that applies to actual existing people – a difficult point, but not one to stay any theoretician who has reached it.

Now, the general fantasy: the extension of the universe. Rather a large undertaking. Let's make it smaller: the preservation, say, of our spiral arm when the galactic core is exploding. A force shield is created about the arm. To provide that, the past is drained of energy. The jewels of Manganon night and day are this force shield, flourescing under the bombardment of the nonthermal radiation from the synchrotron the core has become. Manganon, instead of being parallel with linear time is at right angles to it, co-temporal with their time. One could go on. But why bother? The fantasy has been made smaller, not less improbable. You ask me what to believe. Whatever you like. I favour thought rather than belief.

III

SANDAGE: Let us consider the matter from a totally different angle. Let us explore a concept touched on simply to pass over: the concept of Dendrite and Axon Gates, the comparison with the nerve cell and the nervous system. Now the Gates, qua Gates, are for all their technologically advanced nature, simple things. They get one from A to B, renovating one in the process. That in itself is a huge assumption, but I'll make it. Therefore the gates are not in themselves a nervous system. The analogy breaks down. The messages – if they exist – are concealed from us.

Now I do suggest that Manganon is a nervous system, a brain, and perhaps ultimately a mind, that messages exist, and that their concealment is by an old technique – that of the purloined letter. We, people, are the messages. Not abstractly, symbolically, but literally. Free agents, but messages: an element of acausality introduced into mind. This is hard to grasp. I can see you think I hide behind words. I do not, but reality does. If message impulses are free agents, then the composite is at least acausal with respect to structure. But I see I cannot usefully continue at this time.

GWINDALF: I adhere to the despair philosophy. *They*, discovering time travel, saw their own doom, and despaired. Not completely enough to yield outright, but enough to lose that confidence needed to confront and confound that doom. So they chose to recruit the vigour of their past to confront that doom for them. These in their turn now saw and despaired, and adopted the same technique. And so on . . .

THE END

THE SHIP WHO SANG BY ANNE McCAFFREY

The brain was perfect, the tiny, crippled body useless. So technology rescued the brain and put it in an environment that conditioned it to live in a different kind of body – a spaceship. Here the human mind, more subtle, infinitely more complex than any computer ever devised, could be linked to the massive and delicate strengths, the total recall, and the incredible speeds of space. But the brain behind the ship was entirely feminine – a complex, loving, strong, weak, gentle, savage – a personality, all-woman, called Helva . . .

o 552 10163 X   80p

RESTOREE BY ANNE McCAFFREY

There was a sudden stench of a dead sea creature . . .
There was the horror of a huge black shape closing over her . . .
There was nothing . . .
Then there were pieces of memory . . . isolated fragments that were so horrible her mind refused to accept them . . . intense heat and shivering cold . . . excruciating pain . . . dismembered pieces of the human body . . . sawn bones and searing screams . . .
And when she awoke she found she was in a world that was not earth, and with a face and body that were not her face and body. She had become a Restoree . . .

o 552 10161 3   75p

THIS IS THE WAY THE WORLD BEGINS
BY J. T. McINTOSH

From the holiday planet of Paradiso one could go on many exciting tours and excursions – Mars, Venus, the Moon, even the most distant and alien worlds were accessible to the inquisitive holidaymaker, courtesy of Starways Inc. – the giant combine which owned Paradiso and over half the galaxy.

But of all Starways illustrious trips, there was really only one which interested Ram Burrell – the one which Starways seemed to actually discourage people from taking . . . the trip to planet Earth.

0 552 10432 9   70p

WILL-O-THE-WISP BY THOMAS BURNETT SWANN

Will-o-the-wisp – the light that danced across the Devon moors – enticing the good puritan people to death and devilment . . . For up on the tors dwelt the infamous Gubbings who crucified their victims, murdered and bewitched . . .

Were they really warlocks, or where they creatures of fantasy from another time, another planet?

Robert Herrick, poet, vicar and pagan, the golden giant with a lusty heart, dared to brave the moors and challenge the ancient myth . . .

0 552 10358 6   60p

A SELECTED LIST OF
CORGI SCIENCE FICTION
FOR YOUR READING PLEASURE

All these books are available at your bookshop or newsagent, or can be ordered direct from the publisher. Just tick the titles you want and fill in the form below.